WHEN THE
MARQUESS FALLS

Also by Lorraine Heath

WHEN THE MARQUESS FALLS

LORRAINE HEATH

AVONIMPULSE
An Imprint of HarperCollinsPublishers

An excerpt from *An Affair With a Notorious Heiress* copyright © 2017 by Jan Nowasky.

WHEN THE MARQUESS FALLS. Copyright © 2017 by Jan Nowasky. All rights reserved. Printed in the United States of America. No part of this book may be used or reproduced in any manner whatsoever without written permission except in the case of brief quotations embodied in critical articles and reviews. For information, address HarperCollins Publishers, 195 Broadway, New York, NY 10007.

Digital Edition MARCH 2017 ISBN: 978-0-06-249687-4
Print Edition ISBN: 978-0-06-249688-1

Avon Impulse and the Avon Impulse logo are registered trademarks of HarperCollins Publishers in the United States of America.
Avon and HarperCollins are registered trademarks of HarperCollins Publishers in the United States of America and other countries.

FIRST EDITION

17 18 19 20 21   HDC   10 9 8 7 6 5 4 3 2 1

In loving memory of my parents

My Dear Readers,

If you've read The Viscount and the Vixen, then you know how this story ends. As I was writing that book, however, I found myself wanting to share the Marquess of Marsden's story with more than the snippets that appeared whenever he reminisced about his Linnie. I wanted to bring you the story of a love that was truly undying. Fortunately, my wonderful editor and Avon Books were willing to let me write a very different type of romance.

If you haven't read The Viscount and the Vixen, then I invite you on a journey toward a very special happily ever after.

In either case, I hope you'll enjoy reading this unusual love story.

Wishing you waltzes in the moonlight,
Lorraine

PROLOGUE

Havisham Hall, Devonshire
Early Fall 1834

George William St. John, sixth Marquess of Marsden, ran so hard and so fast that he thought his heart might burst through his chest. In his dozen years upon this earth, he'd never hated anyone as much as he despised all the people who were talking, laughing, and carrying on as though nothing were amiss. Decked out in mourning black, reminding him of scrawny crows, they were all supposed to be as sad as he was, sad that his father was dead. Certainly they'd been solemn at the church and during the funeral procession, and the ladies were consoling his mother. But the gents were drinking his father's spirits and having a jolly good time.

It wasn't to be tolerated. As he was now the marquess, he should make them stop. But his mother had told him that he had to be polite—even to his blasted cousin Robbie who had reminded him that he was next in line should George up and die. He had no plans to do any such thing, especially in the arms of a tavern wench as his father had.

No one was supposed to know that tidbit of information, not even him, but he'd overheard the servants gleefully whispering about it. He didn't like them either. All he wanted was to be alone. He slammed against the oak tree and let flow the tears that had been building ever since his mother informed him that his father was dead. They were accompanied by huge, gulping sobs that shook his shoulders and thin frame. He hated them, too. At the moment he hated everything, decided he always would.

Gathering himself together, he swiped away the embarrassing dampness from his cheeks, inhaled a deep breath, and looked up at the sky. Or wanted to. The view of it was obstructed by the abundance of leaves, the bit of white muslin draped over a branch, and a pair of swaying legs. It was a stupid girl.

"Hello," she called down.

"I wasn't crying," he blurted out, detesting that his voice sounded froggy and hoarse.

"I know. Why don't you come up?"

His mother forbade him to climb trees, forbade him to do a lot of things. "I can't."

"Are you afraid? Don't be scared. You'll like it up here."

It was embarrassing to have a girl think him cowardly. He was the heir. He grimaced. Not anymore. Now he was the marquess. He should be able to do what he wanted. So up he climbed.

As he neared the branch upon which she was sitting, she scooted over to make room for him.

"I'm sorry about your father," she said, once he was settled. He wasn't surprised she knew who he was. Everyone knew who he was.

"Who are you?"

"Linnie, the baker's daughter."

From the village. He'd passed through it on occasion, but he'd never been inside any of the shops. His mother liked only London shops. His father, on the other hand, was apparently fonder of the village offerings, not that he'd ever taken George with him.

"I'm eight years old," she continued on as though her age were important, "and I'm never going to marry."

"How do you know?"

"Because I don't want to." Taking a deep breath, she looked away from him. "It'll be dark soon. I love the night."

He decided she probably loved everything, but then her father wasn't dead.

"You're so lucky to live here," she said. "It's so pretty and your home is monstrously large. I like looking at it."

His mother didn't fancy it, but then she didn't fancy a lot of things. He didn't think she'd even fancied her husband.

"Do you want to talk about him?" she asked.

"Who?"

"Your father."

He shook his head.

She wrapped her hand around his. "It's all right then. We'll just sit here and be quiet."

And so they did. While the shadows began to lengthen and creep over the land, while the sun slowly slid beyond the horizon, while the breeze blew and grew cooler.

"I have to go," she finally said as twilight hovered, and he wished she hadn't broken the spell that had helped him to forget his anger, and his sadness, and his worry.

"Go on." She nudged his arm. "Climb down."

Down. He hadn't considered how he'd get out of the tree when he'd hauled up it, and peering down from his perch now, he realized how very far he'd climbed. The earth, the safety of firm ground, was miles and miles away. "I can't." His voice was an embarrassing squeak.

"All right then, I'll go first."

She scrambled lithely over his lap as though she feared nothing at all. When she reached the trunk, she stretched out her leg and balanced one foot on a lower branch before meeting his gaze, reaching out and squeezing his hand in reassurance. "Keep your eyes on me. I won't let you fall."

It was stupid, but he believed her, believed she had the power to guide him down. So he followed, slowly, tentatively, inch by terrifying inch, looking down into her blue eyes while she gazed up into his of green—until his feet landed on the earth.

"I'll see you around!" she cried, and off she went, darting toward the road that led to the nearby village.

With a measure of wonderment, he watched her go. He might be only twelve, but within the past hour, he'd fallen in love and he knew without question that one day he would marry her.

CHAPTER 1

Devonshire
1847

"I despise it when our mothers get conspiratorial," the Duke of Ashebury lamented, lounging in a chair at a corner table in the Fox and Hare. "Who hosts a ball in the country on Christmas Eve? I've a good mind not to attend."

"They'd leave off if we were married, but we're not."

"State the obvious, why don't you, Greyling?" the Marquess of Marsden asked, although his focus was not entirely on the conversation. Rather he was watching the barmaid with the braid of blond hair circling her head, and the efficient way she swayed her slender hips to avoid wandering hands. He was having a difficult time tamping down his frustration and anger that anyone at all would dare touch her.

"Tupped her yet?" the Earl of Greyling asked, garnering a heated scowl from Marsden.

"We are friends, nothing more."

"That doesn't mean you can't tup her. She works in a tavern. And from a certain angle, she's rather fetching. Maybe I'll have a go at her."

The fury that shot through him had him clenching his jaw until his words could merely slither out. "Only if you wish to lose your teeth."

"You can't imagine she's a virgin."

He not only imagined it, he was rather certain of it. Linnie, the baker's daughter, was not without morals.

Carrying four tankards, two in each hand, she wended her way between the tables, laughing as she went as though she was having a jolly good time. If she had a free hand, she'd no doubt be swatting at the gents who were bold enough to swipe at her backside as she passed. He was of a mind to break a few fingers, a few noses, a few jaws. Fiercely independent, she wouldn't care for the direction of his thoughts. Still he felt an overwhelming need to protect her. She was far too naive to be working in a place such as this.

With a saucy smile, her blue eyes twinkling with mischief, Linnie ambled up to their table, leaned over to present an innocent view of her cleavage revealed by the low cut of her bodice, placed two tankards in front of him, and one each before Ashebury and Greyling. "There you are, lads. Figured you were about due for another pint." She winked at Marsden. "Smile, Georgie. It's Christmas, and you look all grumpy."

"It's not yet Christmas," he groused. They had a week to go. His friends had arrived only that afternoon so they could catch up on the happenings in each others' lives before the dreaded ball.

"'Tis the season. Drink up now and be merry."

With a flourish, she spun on her heel and headed back to the barkeep to fetch someone else's round, effectively dodging wayward hands. The later into the night they got, the bolder the men became. Animals all. It didn't matter that some were aristocrats. They were behaving like heathens.

"She certainly shows a familiarity when speaking to you," Greyling mused, a teasing edge to his tone that irritated, but then it seemed everything tonight was irritating Marsden. "Are you certain you haven't tupped her?"

"Not that it's any of your concern, but it's not as though I'd forget it if I had." On the contrary. It would be a memory he'd carry with him until he drew his last breath. It was an act he'd imagined often enough. He experienced shame every time he did but he seemed incapable of warding off the wayward thoughts. She was deserving of so much more than providing the spark for a man's lustful fantasies.

"Someone's going to," Greyling predicted, and Marsden's ire rose.

"She's a barmaid, not a light skirt."

"Leave off, Greyling," Ashebury ordered. He wasn't shy about using his rank to order them about. It had been that way since Eton. "Besides, we have a more pressing issue to discuss: how to avoid the marriage noose. My mother wants my betrothal for Christmas, and she believes it will happen during the ball at Havisham. She's counting on it as a matter of fact, as is yours and Marsden's. They've practically advertised it as the evening that the Undecided Lords decide."

"The Undecided Lords." Greyling scoffed. "Why must they come up with monikers for us? I am not in the least undecided. I've very much decided that I'm not going to marry before I'm forty."

"It's because our fathers died rather young and left behind only one heir each that they worry." Marsden picked up the tankard Linnie had left behind and downed a good portion of its bitter contents. "We must see to the bloodline."

Ashebury sighed. "Not a very romantic reason to marry."

"At least they're letting us choose our bride," Greyling said. "I've no doubt our fathers would have already arranged a pairing."

A scream followed by ribald laughter had Marsden jerking his attention back to the crowd filling the tavern. He saw Linnie sitting in a bloke's lap, pushing on his shoulders while he seemed intent on planting a kiss on her mouth. Before he was even aware of it, he was halfway across the room with his hands balled at his sides. "Robbie!"

The large, broad man looked over and grinned like an idiot who apparently didn't recognize an avenging angel when he saw one. "Cousin!"

"Release her immediately."

"We're just having a bit of sport. She don't mind, do you, love?"

She shoved hard enough to nearly topple over the chair. "Let me up, you clod."

"First, give us a kiss."

"You're going to be kissing my fist, Robbie," Marsden declared with enough vehemence that those sitting at the table with his daft relation pushed back their chairs as though fearing they might be in the path of the blow.

"Don't be ruining the fun, Cousin."

Marsden moved in, wrapped his arm around Linnie's waist, and extricated her from the oaf's lap. "Off with you."

"Yes, *m'lord*." A tart edge to her voice alerted him that he'd somehow managed to anger her with his rescue, or perhaps it was the command he'd given at the end. She'd never liked him ordering her about even when it was for her own good.

Robbie glowered at him. "You're not the king around here."

"No, I'm the marquess. This village and the villagers are under my protection."

His cousin rolled eyes as green as his. "This isn't medieval England."

"My estate and land give me a responsibility. You are a guest at Havisham, and, therefore, I expect you to behave as a gentleman while you are in the area." He didn't know why his mother had invited his cousin to come for Christmas unless it was to remind him of who would inherit if he didn't provide an heir. Robbie's father had served as Marsden's guardian after his own father died. His entire family had lived at Havisham. Marsden had never been so glad in his life as he was when he reached his majority and could kick the lot out. He'd settled a generous amount on his former guardian that had allowed him to purchase a small estate. He wished only that it was located farther away, preferably in another country.

Robbie shoved himself to his feet. "What are you going to do if I'm not?"

"I'll flatten you." God, he wanted to. He'd wanted to ever since he was six years old, and Robbie, three years his senior, had tossed him into a pigpen to wallow in the muck.

Robbie glared at him, then looked past him, shrugged. "I was just having a bit of fun." He dropped into his chair. "A concept with which you are obviously unfamiliar. But no matter. I'm content to merely drink." He lifted his tankard and began gulping down the contents.

Marsden didn't quite trust him, but still he turned around and came up short at the sight of his two friends standing mere inches behind him.

"I was hoping for a round of fisticuffs," Greyling said.

"We could take the whole lot of them out," Ashebury assured him.

"I think they'll behave now." And if not, then he and his friends would deal with them, which would be far easier than dealing with Linnie when the time came.

H er swollen feet hurt and her back ached, but Madeline Connor simply put away the broom and rags she and the other lasses had used to clean up after the last of the customers left. She got in the queue, waited her turn, and smiled at the tavern keeper and proprietor as he placed the coins in her hand. Nothing she liked better than the tinkling of silvers and coppers hitting each other, even if it was only three of them.

"'Night, Henry. See you tomorrow."

"Take care, Linn."

She snatched her cloak from a peg on the wall, draped it over her shoulders, and walked out into the cold night, her heart giving a little lurch as a man shoved himself away from the wall. Then she recognized him and her temper flared. "What are you doing here?"

"I'm going to walk you home," the Marquess of Marsden said.

With a roll of her eyes, she began striding up the street. "I get myself home every night just fine when you're not about."

"But I'm about now, and I know you're upset with me. Do you fancy Robbie? Were you flirting with him?"

If she were ten years younger, she'd smack him on the shoulder, but as it was, she merely scoffed. "No, he's a buffoon. A drunk one at that. But I can take care of myself."

"I don't know why you have to work there."

"My da gives me a roof over my head for working in the bakery. The pub puts coins in my pocket so I can move to London and open my own bakery."

"London has enough bakeries."

She nudged her shoulder against his arm—hard—causing him to stumble. "Don't spit on my dream."

Straightening, he tugged on his gloves when they already appeared to be snugly in place. "You won't like London. It's foul-smelling and crowded."

She could do without the odor, but an abundance of people suited her, because she could become lost, might never again see him. "You seem to spend enough time there."

"Not by choice. I much prefer it here."

Stopping, she leaned against a wall. It was late, no one was about except for a stray dog or two. "And why is that, m'lord?"

He glanced around before stepping nearer to her. She held her breath, waiting for the words she longed to hear. *Because you're here.*

"It's my home." His voice, deep in the quiet, wrapped around her. She'd teased him unmercifully when it began to deepen, often cracking as though uncertain in which direction it wished to go: high or low.

But now her heart tightened, squeezed, dropped to her toes. How could he not see that she loved him, that she couldn't stay here once he married, and he'd be marrying before the next year was out if his mother had her way. Linnie knew all about the blasted ball and its purpose: to secure him a wife. She needed to be long gone before a beautiful noble-woman took up residence at Havisham Hall.

"Well, it's not mine." She shoved herself away from the wall and began marching with determination.

He was quick to catch up. "What do you mean it's not yours? You live here. Your family is here."

"My da. And he's getting up in years. What do I do when he's gone?"

"You take over his bakery. Why go to London when you have a shop here?"

"I'm in the mood for something different, some excite-ment—"

"Then come to the Havisham ball."

She staggered to a stop and swung around to face him. For years, from the shadows, she'd watched the fancy folk arrive and promenade through the gardens. Once she'd even snuck up to the windows of the grand residence to see them dancing in the magnificent ballroom. "Don't be daft, George. I'm a commoner."

"You're anything but common. It'll be my Christmas gift to you. A night of merriment and excitement."

She wasn't half tempted. To be part of something so much grander than herself and her village life was something she sometimes dreamed about—before the reality of her situation anchored her back to the real circumstances of her place in the world. "What would I wear?"

His brow furrowed. "Well, a gown of course."

Said so simply by a man for whom everything came so easily. She didn't resent his place in the world but sometimes it did give him a skewed perspective of what surviving entailed for others. "I don't have a gown, not like the ones they wear to your glamorous affairs."

"Then we shall simply have to send to London for one." He glanced around, before taking her arm and ushering her into the narrow alley between two taverns. This village had more than its share of drunkards. "Please come. It's going to be a dreadfully dull affair."

"You just told me it would be exciting."

"It will be if you're there."

She lowered her gaze to his perfectly knotted cravat. He hadn't buttoned his outer coat. She wanted to step into him, feel his warmth as he closed the heavy wool around her. Lifting her eyes, she touched his cheek, skimming the back of her fingers over his bristled jaw. For the most part, his features were lost to the shadows, but she didn't need to see them to know them. "Your mother wouldn't like it and neither would the lady you're courting."

"I'm not courting anyone."

"But I've heard rumors you'll decide that night whom you should court." Whom he would marry. Her stomach knotted with the acknowledgment that soon he would no longer belong to her in any fashion whatsoever. "My presence would serve as a distraction."

"You could help me determine who is best suited to me."

Oh, yes, she bloody well wanted to do that. "Don't be daft, George. You know best who will make you happy."

He removed his gloves and cradled her face between his large warm hands. His palms were smooth, not rough like her father's. Still she felt strength in his fingers. "And if I can't have her?"

"You could kiss her." She'd wanted that for as long as she could remember. A silly thing for a silly girl to wish for. He was the lord of the manor, far beyond her reach.

She went completely still as he leaned in, his breath fanning over her cheek. "And if I can't stop there?"

"She'll stop you before it goes too far."

With his thumbs, he stroked the corners of her mouth. "A gentleman does not take advantage."

"Do you want to kiss me?"

"More than I want to breathe. I have for the longest."

She couldn't help but grin at the need echoing through his tone. "Then why haven't you?"

"My world would not accept you."

"Then don't tell them."

His laugh was a rush of air as he pressed his forehead to hers. "It would be wrong when I can't give you promises."

"Where's the harm in a kiss?"

Rising up on her toes, she tentatively pressed her lips to his, heard his low groan as he flattened his body against hers. With his tongue, he lapped insistently at the seam of her mouth until she opened for him—and her words mocked her.

She could see the harm in it now, feel the harm in it as heat swamped her and their tongues became entangled, exploring, tasting, very nearly devouring. God help her, but she had waited years for this moment, had started to crave it as her body transformed from girl into woman. No other boy had ever appealed to her as he had. But when his voice had deepened and he'd grown tall and his shoulders had broadened and whiskers had shadowed his jaw, strange stirrings had begun in the pit of her stomach and lower. She'd wanted his hands on her, on all of her.

Now she wrapped her fingers around his wrist and carried the hand that cupped her face down, slipping it beneath her cloak until it cradled her breast. His guttural growl was the most enticing sound she'd ever heard. He kneaded the pliant orb, his thumb circling her turgid nipple. The pleasure that rippled through her nearly had her knees buckling.

She didn't think it was possible for him to get any closer, but she became aware of the movement of his hips as he rubbed his hard cock against the apex of her thighs. Ah, yes, there was danger in a kiss, in his at least. She wanted to lift her skirts, to have him even nearer, to have him dragging his cock between the folds that harbored secrets she'd dared not even think about.

He deepened the kiss as though it provided sustenance, as though it alone ensured survival.

"Madeline."

Marsden reacted to the sharply delivered word more quickly than she did. She was dizzy, breathless, and only his hands moving to her waist kept her aloft, prevented her from sinking to the ground and urging him to follow her down.

"Mr. Connor," Marsden said, the rasp of his voice slipping into her soul.

Blinking, striving to regain her equilibrium, she saw her protective father standing there, an ominous sentinel in the night. He'd obviously come looking for her when she didn't arrive home as expected. "Papa—"

"Off with you now, Madeline," he said brusquely.

She looked at Marsden. He merely nodded and stepped away. It irritated her that he looked guilty doing it. Angling her chin, she met her father's gaze, hoping the darkness hid from him the flush burning her cheeks. "It was only a kiss."

"It's never only a kiss," her father said. "Go on."

"Good night, George," she said.

"Good night, Miss Connor." He always addressed her in

that manner when it wasn't only the two of them. Tonight it irked beyond all measure.

Marching away from both men, she heard her father's voice but not his words. Then his rapid footsteps as he caught up to her.

"He won't marry you." She heard the truth and the sadness in his tone. "He's nobility, and you're a baker's daughter."

"I know."

But what she knew in her head was very different from what she believed in her heart.

CHAPTER 2

"Don't ruin her, m'lord. If you do, you'll also ruin her life."

Connor's parting words echoed through Marsden's head as he galloped back to Havisham, handed his horse over to the stable boy, strode into the residence, and headed for the stairs. Damn it, he knew the truth of them which was the reason he'd resisted the lure of Linnie for so long, but then tonight seeing her with Robbie—

When she had asked, "Where is the harm?" he'd merely planned to explain all the ways in which it existed. But when she'd pressed her lips to his, all the fantasies he'd harbored over the years finally were presented with the opportunity to exist in reality. She felt so damned good, smelled so intoxicating. The warmth, the sighs, the feel of her in his arms—

"You're home at last, I see."

He swung around. His mother—who had obviously come from the parlor—stood stiffly before him, appearing none too happy, but then she was not generally a jolly sort.

"Your friends returned over an hour ago." Her voice rang with admonishment as though he were still a lad to be chastised rather than a full-grown man who now managed estates and mines.

"I had a matter to which I needed to attend."

"You can't marry a baker's daughter."

He didn't know how she knew—probably Robbie, on further thought. No telling what tales his cousin had told upon arriving at the residence after the tavern closed. "I wasn't taking her to Gretna Green. I was escorting her home."

"It was one thing for you to spend time with the chit when you were children. It's entirely inappropriate now that you're a grown man with responsibilities."

"Friendship does not end when one reaches a certain age. Besides, Robbie attempted to take advantage of her this evening so I felt it was my duty to ensure she reached home safely."

"He told me that you threatened to strike him. I don't know why you and your cousin are always at odds."

"Perhaps because he's an ass."

"Your language!"

He merely shook his head. "Good night, Mother." He turned to go—

"I'm not finished speaking with you."

With an exasperated sigh, he faced her. She was fairly seething with righteous indignation, but then it wasn't the first time they'd squared off thusly. "I will not have you behaving as your father did, taking up with the lowest of women and bringing shame to this house—"

"Linnie is not like the women with whom Father associated. She works hard, she asks nothing of me." Except for a kiss and that could have led to disaster if her father hadn't shown up. Marsden had been on the cusp of securing them a room in one of the taverns. He'd never wanted anything as much as he'd wanted to be closer to her, with no clothes separating his skin from hers. He'd wanted to taste every inch of her, not only her lips. He'd wanted to know her in a way that would have been wrong on so many levels when he couldn't offer her his name.

"If she gets with child, you cannot marry her and ladies of quality frown on bastards running around."

He rolled his eyes at the ludicrousness of this conversation. His mother distrusted all men. It irked that she also distrusted her son. "Not that it is any of your business but we have not had nor will we have carnal relations. I have too much respect for her to take advantage. We are what we have been since we were children: friends."

As though gratified to hear that, she relaxed somewhat and extended a sheaf of paper. "Good. Now, I have managed to reduce the number of girls attending the ball to a list of half a dozen you should consider as a future wife."

Ah, yes, what every gent wanted: a woman selected by his mother. Still, he took the list, glanced over it quickly. He knew most but not all the names.

"They would each make an exceptional marchioness," his mother stated.

He had no doubt there as his mother had very exacting requirements, but he wasn't of a mind to give her what she wanted so easily, not when she'd done all in her power through the years to discourage his friendship with Linnie. "You're to invite Miss Connor to the ball."

"The baker's daughter!" Her shrill shriek would no doubt awaken the staff. "You are *not* considering her for a wife."

"No, but I want her to attend the ball." Having caught her once peering in through the windows, he knew she longed to be part of the festivities. Besides, he'd already invited her.

"Don't be ridiculous. She doesn't belong here."

He held up the paper. "Do you wish for me to consider one of these ladies for matrimony?"

"Of course I do. I wouldn't have gone to the trouble of listing them otherwise."

"Then you will send an invitation to Madeline Connor. You will welcome her into this residence as though she were related to the queen. You will send to London for your seamstress and ensure she has a proper gown to wear."

"The ball is in less than a sennight. My seamstress cannot work miracles."

"And here I thought it was the season for such."

His mother glared at him. "You're being preposterous."

"Still, if you want your ball to be as you've touted it with at least one of the Undecided Lords deciding then you shall have an invitation for Linnie waiting on my desk in the morning so I may deliver it in the afternoon. Otherwise, I might find myself spending the evening of the ball in the village, deep into my cups."

"Why do you despise me so?"

He gave her a gentle smile. "I don't despise you, but I do loathe those among us who consider others beneath us simply because of the circumstances of their birth. Sleep well."

Although as he turned for the stairs, he doubted she'd sleep at all. Rather she'd seethe all night regarding his demands, but he'd be damned if he wasn't going to spend as much time as possible with Linnie when it might turn out to be his last Christmas with her.

They only kept the shop open until half past two, which gave Linnie an opportunity to catch a few winks before heading to the tavern. But when she opened her bakery in London she was going to keep the doors unlocked until sunset. Surely, Londoners had a more leisurely life and would make their purchases later in the afternoon. She would also have a delivery service for the fancy and the posh. She had all sorts of plans to ensure her business supported her and allowed her to set aside funds for her old age. Her da, bless his heart, would probably be working until the day he cocked up his toes. As for herself, she wanted to have a bit more fun before she went to her grave.

The bell above the door tinkled as it opened, and her heart lurched at the sight of Marsden strolling inside, removing his hat in one fluid motion. How was it that he encompassed both gracefulness and masculinity? After being caught in a compromising position the night before, she hadn't expected

him to be so bold as to appear here when he knew her father would be about.

"M'lord," she said as he neared the counter, although he had yet to look at her directly but seemed more interested in the few loaves that remained on the shelves behind the glass.

"Are we going to be formal today, Miss Connor?" he asked, bending slightly to study the pumpernickel.

"It's advisable." She leaned over the counter slightly and whispered, "My father's in the kitchens."

"Then I shall be on my best behavior."

And his best obviously involved giving his attention to the baked dough. Irritated with his ignoring her, she heaved a sigh. "Why are you here, George?"

"I'm in need of bread for a picnic."

"In winter? One doesn't picnic in the cold. Are you daft?"

He peered up at her then. "Does one not?"

"No, one does not unless he wishes to catch his death."

"I think one can. Perhaps I'll show you sometime."

She wished he would. "I don't think that would be w

Finally, he straightened. "We spent more time tog
when we were younger. Chasing after each other, f
climbing trees. I even taught you to ride a horse."

"All in innocence. We lose our innocence as we g

"Indeed we do. I enjoyed kissing you."

The heat suffused her face. "You'd best not let
hear you say that."

"Did you like kissing me?"

She shook her head, surprised when he suddenly looked devastated. "It ended too soon, but until then—" She shrugged. "I have no complaints."

He grinned. "I think you enjoyed it more than I did."

"It was more involved than I expected it to be." She'd especially liked the lovely way he'd fondled her breast, wish he'd had time to give attention to the other.

"Was it your first?" he asked.

She nodded. "Yours?"

He shook his head. "No."

Jealousy speared her. He was four years older. It was ridiculous to think he'd have had the patience to wait for her to grow up. "Was she pretty?"

"I don't recall. I suppose I should but I was quite foxed at the time."

"Have you done more than kiss?"

He held her gaze until she wanted to squirm. They'd never had any difficulty discussing the most intimate of things but she was beginning to wish she hadn't asked.

"I have," he finally said quietly.

"What was it like?" she whispered.

"Awkward. I was clumsy and rather . . . quick. I doubt the entire exchange lasted as long as our kiss last night."

Her eyes widened. "I thought copulating lasted all night."

"I suspect on occasion it could."

"Not very ladylike of me to ask, I suppose. But then I'm really a lady, am I?"

"I've always told you that you can ask me anything."

As you can ask me."

"Good." He looked back down at the shelves. "Which is your favorite bread, as I need to purchase a loaf."

"Sourdough." She grabbed one, wrapped it in paper, and handed it to him. "I'll add it to your account."

"Very good."

"Afternoon, m'lord."

Linnie rolled her eyes at her father's resounding voice echoing around them. He sounded less happy than he had the night before.

"Good afternoon, Mr. Connor." Marsden held up his purchase. "I needed some bread."

"I should think your cook would provide that."

"We have an abundance of guests arriving, and I didn't wish to trouble her when my need is personal. And I almost forgot. I needed to deliver this." He reached into his coat pocket, removed an ivory vellum envelope, and extended it toward her. "On behalf of my mother."

Why the devil would Lady Marsden send a missive? The woman had never spoken to Linnie except to chastise her when she was younger and had been tearing through the garden, Marsden hot on her heels. Taking it, she stared at it as though it were an unknown object. *Miss Madeline Connor* was written in delicate script.

"You should open it," Marsden insisted. "It might require a response."

"Yes, of course." With care, she unsealed the envelope and removed another vellum piece, only this one was embossed with gold lettering, requesting her presence at the ball. "She can't be serious." She looked up at him. "This is a prank."

"She's deadly serious. Her seamstress will be arriving in a couple of days to create your gown. I'll send a carriage for you the night of the ball."

"I can't go."

"Why not?"

"I'll stick out like a sore thumb."

"Too scared? Cowardly? Afraid?"

"This isn't the same as climbing a tree. And we're not children to taunt each other."

"It's exactly like it. You've always wanted to attend one of her balls; I know you have. It's my Christmas gift to you. Before you head off to your new life in London. I'll let her know you've graciously accepted."

"You'll do no such thing."

"You should go to the ball," her father said.

Pivoting on her heel, she stared at him. "You can't think this is a good idea."

"You need to understand where you belong."

"I know where I belong." But he was correct. Knowing she could never scale into societal heights didn't make her want Marsden any less. So she gave his Lordship a curt nod. "Let your mother know I look forward to it."

"I shall look forward to our dance. Your first shall belong to me."

With that he walked out of the shop. She trailed her fingers over the raised lettering.

"Best to let him break your heart now while you're young enough to recover," her father said.

"Did it never occur to you that I might break his?"

"Not once. You need to understand, Madeline, that to his kind, you are merely a plaything."

Leaving her with that unsettling thought, he retreated to the kitchen. He didn't understand that for some, being a plaything was better than being nothing at all.

CHAPTER 3

Linnie stared at the gorgeous emerald green gown spread out over her bed. She was stunned by how quickly and efficiently the seamstress had worked and how rapidly the days had passed. Countless times she'd told herself she wouldn't attend the ball but now that the moment was here, that it was the eve of Christmas, the notion of not going filled her with a profound sadness. She'd never again have the opportunity to attend such a grand affair.

As soon as she could, she'd move to London and open her bakery. She'd never again see Marsden or have a chance to dance with him.

The tavern keeper had given her the night off. Most of the gents would be with their families tonight and the other girls could handle the few who weren't. She hadn't told her friends about the invitation to the great manor, hadn't wanted them thinking she was putting on airs. Besides, she didn't have many friends, as most of the villagers assumed she was more than friends with Marsden. She'd never told him because she feared he'd get angry and make matters worse. Or maybe she was afraid he wouldn't get angry at all. That her father was right. That she was little more than an amusement to the lord of the manor.

Perhaps tonight *was* designed to confirm her place in this world, as though she didn't already know it. Only if that was the case, it was the marchioness's scheme, not her son's. Linnie trusted Marsden, always had. Still she wavered. Was it best to step into his world for only a night or never to have stepped into it at all?

He'd questioned her bravery just as she'd done his when they first met, when she'd egged him into climbing the tree. If she didn't go she'd be angrier at herself than at him.

The soft knock nearly made her jump out of her skin. No doubt her father coming to issue an abundance of warnings, but when she opened the door he was standing there with a young dark-haired woman who couldn't have been much older than Linnie herself.

She curtsied. "Miss, I'm Sarah Barnaby. His Lordship sent me to help you dress and to serve as your chaperone."

"At least he's going to take care with your reputation," her father said.

With that he headed down the hallway to the main living area above the shop. She turned back to the girl. "Come in, Miss Barnaby."

"Oh, you must call me Sarah. I'm merely one of the parlor maids."

"Then you must call me Linnie."

"I couldn't be so informal."

"We're not that different."

"You're attending her Ladyship's ball. I'll never get to do that." The girl stepped into the room. "Caw, blimey! Is that your gown?"

"It is, yes."

"It's gorgeous." She pivoted around. "I can put up your hair for you."

"That would be lovely, thank you."

"Let's get to it, shall we?"

An hour later, Linnie stood before the mirror admiring her reflection. She'd never considered herself much to look at, but the green gown was the perfect shade for her complexion, and had the added pleasure of matching Marsden's eyes. What a silly girl she was to care about that. Sarah had pinned up her hair and left curling tendrils to frame her face.

"Oh, I forgot," the maid said. "His Lordship told me to give you this." She removed a leather box from the pocket of her skirt.

Linnie had never seen such a gorgeous package and was a bit nervous about what it might contain. When she opened it, she saw that her trepidation was justified. A gold chain was threaded through an emerald shaped like a teardrop. "I can't accept this."

But oh, how she wanted to.

"You must. I'll get in trouble otherwise. His Lordship might think I nicked it."

"I'll make sure he knows the truth of it."

"You should at least try it on."

"No harm in that, I suppose." Only once it was on, she didn't want to remove it. It was the perfect accompaniment for the gown.

"You should wear it to the ball," Sarah said.

Linnie could do little more than nod as she and the maid left her bedchamber. Her father was waiting for her in the main living area, her heaviest cloak draped over his arm.

"Don't look so worried," she told him. "I'm not going to do anything foolish."

"This that you're doing tonight seems foolish enough to me."

"You encouraged me to go," she reminded him.

"Which no doubt makes us both fools." He held up her cloak. She turned her back to him. As he draped it over her shoulders, he said in a low voice, "You look beautiful, Madeline. You deserve fine things but never forget that they come at a high price."

Swinging around, she rose up on her toes and kissed his cheek. "I'm not my mother." She'd always dreamed of more than a life in the village. One day she had run off with a traveling coppersmith who had sold pots from his wagon.

"It's an easy thing to have one's head turned."

"I know my own mind . . . and my own worth."

"And your heart? Do you know your heart? It can betray us quicker than anything."

"I'll take care, I promise." Even if promises were easily and quickly broken as well.

With the maid in tow, she went down the stairs that led into the kitchens. She inhaled the familiar fragrance of flour, finding strength in it as she carried on through the shop.

Once outside, she locked the door before turning toward the shining black coach and the waiting liveried footman. She felt rather like a princess being ushered to a ball. Havisham wasn't that far away and she'd always simply used her legs to get there.

The footman bowed slightly before opening the door. He handed her up. She nearly screamed at the unexpected company waiting inside. "Jesus, George. What the devil are you doing skulking about in here?"

"I'm not skulking. I have a lantern burning."

She settled onto the bench opposite him. "Why didn't you come inside?"

"I didn't want to endure your father's lectures."

"So you left me to face them alone?"

"Did he lecture you?" Marsden asked.

"Of course he did. He thinks you're up to no good."

Marsden grinned. She loved that smile. "We have more than a hundred guests at Havisham. There will be eyes everywhere. I don't see how we can get into trouble."

"A hundred?" The one ball she'd looked in on had been crowded, but a hundred?

"It's usually more but the weather kept some away. Others like to be at home for Christmas. So most of the guests are young ladies hoping to snag a duke, a marquess, or an earl. Or at the very least find a way to haunt us until the Season begins."

"Your lot has odd courtship rituals. We commoners are a bit more forthright about it."

Sarah eased in beside her. The footman closed the door, and in the next instant the wheels were whirring and the hooves pounding.

"Do you like the necklace?" he asked.

She closed her fingers around the cool emerald. "I'm only borrowing it for the night. I'll return it on the morrow."

"Don't be silly. It's yours." Irritation laced his voice.

"It's too fine a gift, George. You know that. A lady can't accept something like this from a gentleman to whom she isn't married."

"You're not a lady."

Her temper flared. She was on the verge of ordering him to stop the coach when he said, "You're my dearest friend."

He'd always had a knack for dousing her anger. "Still, it wouldn't be appropriate."

"No one has to know. You can say your father gave it to you."

"Oh, yes, because my father can afford something as fine as this. Besides, Sarah knows the truth of it."

"She's not going to say anything. Are you, Sarah?"

"Forgive me, m'lord, but I dunno what you're talkin' about."

He looked as triumphant as he had when they were children and he bested her at something. "There. It'll be our secret."

"I'll consider it. By the by, how in the devil did you convince your mother to invite me? In all the years you and I have been friends, I don't think she and I have exchanged a dozen words."

He looked out the window. "I merely had to ask her to include you among the guests."

If it had been that simple, he'd still be looking her in the eye. "George?"

"Leave off, Linnie."

"I want to know what giving me tonight cost you."

With a sigh he brought his gaze back to bear on her. She rather wished he'd doused the flame in the lamp. Before he even spoke, she knew the price was high.

"I promised to select a wife this evening." Before she could comment on the unfairness of it, he held up a hand. "Or at least decide which woman I would make an effort to court next Season." He shrugged. "Who knows? Perhaps the one I choose won't have me."

"She'd be a fool not to."

He gave her a sad smile. "Ladies like London—all the hustle and bustle of it. It can be quite lonely out on the moors. I prefer the moors."

She didn't want to contemplate that she might not prefer the city either. She couldn't remain here once he married. "Still, you'll take her to London."

"To keep her happy, I suppose I must."

And he would seek to please her. She knew instinctually that he would work to ensure the woman never regretted marrying him.

"You might get lucky, George. Surely you can find a woman who prefers solitude or having all the time alone with her handsome husband that she can imagine."

"You think me handsome?"

With his strong, square draw, his sharp aquiline nose, and his brilliant green eyes, how could he not be? "You have your moments, now that your knees aren't so knobby."

He scowled. "It's been years since I've worn short pants. You have no idea what my knees look like."

"Are you saying they're knobby?"

"Perhaps I'll show them to you and let you judge."

"That would be scandalous."

"I doubt yours are knobby."

"I'm not going to show you."

He chuckled low. "If I could have conversations with other ladies as I have with you, I might not mind securing a wife."

"I think you might be surprised what other ladies are willing to discuss."

The coach rolled to a stop. Excitement and trepidation sliced through her as the door opened. Marsden leaped out, then reached back in, extending his gloved hand to her. She pressed her palm to his, felt his fingers close firmly around hers. They might as well have been encircling her heart. She was a fool to come here, to place herself on the path to temptation. Still, she stepped down, walking toward the large manor, barely aware of the footman assisting Sarah. She'd waited her entire life to be welcomed into the manor. She was going to make the most of it.

She felt the dampness on her cheeks and glanced up. "It's starting to snow."

"Rest assured that I'll see you safely home."

He led her up the steps and through the huge doorway

into the cavernous and impressive foyer, with its marble floor and crystal chandelier. A footman took her wrap and Marsden's coat and hat.

Glancing around, she said, "It makes me feel so small."

When her comment was met with silence, she faced him, surprised to see him staring at her as though he'd never seen her before. "Good Lord, what's wrong? Have my fastenings come undone?"

His gaze sweeping over her, he shook his head. "You're gorgeous."

He was as well, decked out in his evening attire. Women no doubt tripped over themselves hoping to gain his attention. Still his words caused heat to warm her cheeks. She scoffed, laughed self-consciously. "Don't be silly. It's just a fancy frock."

"It's more than the frock." He shrugged, smiled. "I don't know what it is. It's as though this house has been waiting for you or you've been waiting to step into this residence. You fairly shine, Linnie."

"That's a fanciful thought. You're not usually prone to fanciful thoughts."

"No, I'm not. I suppose we should get to the ball. Most people are staying here. They're probably already in the ballroom." He offered his crooked elbow.

She wound her arm around his. They began wandering down a wide hallway. "I've always wondered how your home looked. I don't suppose you could show me some of it later."

"You know what the ballroom looks like. I caught you peering in through the window."

"I was all of fourteen and I barely remember it." She did remember catching glimpses of him waltzing with a young woman. At the time, she'd been certain he'd marry before she could catch up to him. Now she was old enough to marry, but not posh enough for him and his place in the world.

"The cold and the snow will stop us from taking a turn about the garden," he said, "so perhaps we shall take a turn about the house. I'm certain people will be strolling through the portrait gallery."

She wanted to see more than that. She wanted to see everything so years from now, she could imagine him here, with his family, enjoying himself. She did so want him to have a good life.

They began ascending stairs. She could hear music filtering through the walls. Her nervousness ratcheted up a notch. "I don't know how to dance, George."

"It's the gentleman's role to lead you. You'll do fine."

At the top of the stairs, they stepped into a grand salon and stood on a landing that led down to the dance floor. The tall walls were covered in mirrors. The crystal chandeliers sparkled. Even in the dead of winter, flowers adorned decorative tables. Seeing it all from the inside was so much better than viewing it from the outside. The grandeur was something she'd never forget but she couldn't imagine living with it. Something to be appreciated on occasion but certainly not something that would create happiness.

Marsden stepped away, spoke to a footman standing at the edge of the landing, then returned to her side.

"Miss Madeline Connor!" the man bellowed in a deep

voice that echoed through the room, and her heart kicked against her ribs.

Marsden once again offered his arm. As she placed her hand on it, she asked, "Why isn't he announcing you?"

"Because I'm the host. Everyone should know who I am."

Based on the way people were staring, she had a feeling a good many knew who she was. Or least *what* she was. Still, she held her head high and descended with all the grace she could muster. In a wink, she found herself standing before the formidable marchioness.

"Mother, allow me the honor of introducing Miss Madeline Connor," he said, as though she'd never before met his mother. Although to be fair, they'd never been formally introduced.

Linnie dropped into a deep curtsy. "I'm truly honored to have received your kind invitation, Lady Marsden."

The marchioness did a very good imitation of a surprised chicken. "You don't speak like a commoner."

Linnie rose. "Your son gets the credit for that. He was always correcting my articulation when we were younger." Which she thought would serve her well when she moved to London and wanted to meet with bankers or businessmen.

"I see." She glanced over at her son as though she suspected him of engaging in something nefarious. "Well, I hope you'll enjoy the ball."

"I'm certain I will. I've never seen such gaiety. It speaks well of your skill at putting people at ease. It's the sign of a grand lady."

If his mother stood any straighter, Linnie thought her

back might crack. "I am known for being an exceptional hostess."

"I immediately can see the reason for it."

She was aware of music drifting into silence.

"If you'll excuse us, Mother, another tune will be starting up shortly and Miss Connor has promised me her first dance."

"Yes, of course. It was a pleasure, Miss Connor."

Her tone almost had Linnie believing her. "The pleasure was all mine, my lady."

Then, thank goodness, Marsden led her away from the tigress as another tune did indeed begin to fill the air.

"Well done," he whispered near her ear.

"All good tavern wenches know that flattering the gents might earn them an extra coin. I didn't think your mother would be immune to flattery."

"Indeed, she is not."

They reached the area where couples were gliding over the floor, the woman held in the man's arms. Not at all the sort of dancing that went on at the village festival.

"A waltz," Marsden said. "Want to give it a try?"

She smiled up at him. "I do."

And then he was sweeping her into the fray.

Chapter 4

It was a mistake to have invited her to the ball. He'd never be able to walk into the foyer without seeing her there, with appreciation for her surroundings dancing in her eyes. He'd never be able to greet another woman arriving without seeing Linnie in emerald velvet and silk smiling up at him. He would always see her strolling through the hallway at his side, ascending the stairs, descending into the ballroom.

No doubt other balls would be held here, and he would circle the room with other ladies in his arms, but he would always see Linnie, holding his gaze, her face wreathed with joy. He wanted to plow his hands into her hair, ferret out the pins, and send the heavy strands tumbling down her back. He wanted to draw her nearer, allow her orange fragrance to overwhelm his senses until he could no longer smell the tartness of the evergreen boughs that dotted the room.

He'd offered this night as his Christmas gift to her, but

it was for himself as well. If she was relocating to London, he wanted as much time with her as possible before she departed. It had been so much easier when they were younger, before his voice had changed and he'd begun to look upon women differently, before he'd returned from school and noticed changes in her: the rounding of her hips and the remarkable curves of her bosom. The way her smile was a bit saucier. The way she could naïvely tease him with her hand coming to rest on his arm and shoulder. As children, they'd held hands. Now whenever she touched him, albeit innocently, he felt like a piece of kindling ready to ignite, like some wild beast barely tethered. He desperately wanted to break free of all societal restraints and behave like a barbarian, claiming her as his own.

His thoughts regarding her were inappropriate and yet he seemed unable to escape the untoward images of stripping her bare and spreading her out over silk sheets that often taunted him. He'd awaken in the middle of the night, hard and aching, with fantasies of kissing her in secret intimate places racing through his mind. Even now, he seemed incapable of taking his gaze from her, of not falling into the blue depths of her eyes.

"Are the balls in London like this one?" she asked.

"Larger, more people about. Warmer. Doors are often left open to allow for cooler air. And people spend time on the terrace or in the gardens."

"Perhaps I can entice the nobility into purchasing bread for special occasions from my bakery."

He loved her optimism, how often and easily she smiled.

His mother always appeared sour, as though whatever she ate didn't agree with her. "I'll hope so, for the sake of your enterprise."

"You don't think I'm going to do it, move to London."

It would no doubt be best for his marriage if she did. "I think you'll follow your heart."

She averted her gaze; her smile faltered. "Sometimes it's unwise to follow where our heart leads so it's better if we don't."

The music faded away. If she were like the other ladies here, with a mother or chaperone handling a tether, he would escort her off the dance floor and leave her alone. But tonight she was his responsibility, his personal guest, the only lady in whom he had any interest. "Would you care for some champagne?"

Her smile returned and her gaze swung back to his, no evidence of sorrow remaining. "I'd care to try it. I don't know if I'd like it."

While he escorted her to an area where people mingled, he felt numerous eyes following them, could read errant thoughts in the speculative gazes of some of the men. She was a curiosity, an outsider. He wanted to shout, "She is more welcome than all of you!"

As a footman carrying a tray passed by, Marsden snagged two flutes of the bubbling brew and handed her one. He lifted his. "To a night of firsts."

"To the second finest gift you've ever given me."

He furrowed his brow. "What was the first?"

"Your friendship."

She said it so simply, so easily. From the beginning, they had accepted each other as equals, and yet tonight the differences mocked him. He was the lord of the manor and she the baker's daughter, the sometimes tavern wench. Some of the men in this room had slapped her backside, pinched her cheek, made salacious comments about her. She no doubt recognized the offenders, yet she held her head high and ignored them. She was not one to be intimidated. He had no doubt her bakery would be a smashing success. She'd settle for nothing less.

Over the rim of his glass, he watched as she took a small sip, smiled.

"Oh, I like it. The bubbles tickle."

She never took anything for granted, appreciated everything, even the smallest of pleasures.

"Well, if it isn't the tavern maid," Greyling said, suddenly at Marsden's shoulder, Ashebury beside him. "Don't you clean up nicely?"

She tipped up her chin. "I don't recall being dirty."

"It's an expression, m'dear." He nudged Marsden's elbow. "I'm surprised your mother invited a commoner."

"My mother wishes to see me happy."

"She wishes to see you married," Ashebury said, his gaze wandering over Linnie. "And not to her, I'm sure."

"No, not to me," Linnie said.

"I meant no offense, but in our world—"

"You're a lot of pompous asses," she responded with a sugary smile, and Marsden wanted to cheer her on.

Ashebury laughed. "Yes, we are, I'm afraid."

"Have either of you had any luck meeting your mothers' expectations?" Marsden asked, hoping to draw attention away from a conversation that might ruin Linnie's night.

"Not yet," Ashebury admitted, "although I daresay the choices are top notch. The marchioness has discerning tastes."

Ah, yes, his mother's invitations had been dispatched to young, beautiful girls. Ones who came from untarnished bloodlines. Ones whose lineage could be traced back for generations. Ones whose families had the distinction of being listed in *Debrett's*. Ones he and his friends should marry for social status, political gain, influence. Ones who could elevate their positions within Society, or at least ensure their place was maintained. Those among the peerage did not marry for something as trite as love.

"I say, Miss Connor, would you honor me with a dance?" Greyling asked, his offer not only taking Marsden by surprise but causing an emotion quite feral to course through him. It bordered on jealousy even as he knew he had no right to experience such possessiveness when he could only offer her friendship.

She cast a questioning glance his way. He wanted to tell her to decline; he wanted her all for himself but it wasn't fair when tonight was his gift to her, was supposed to give her memories of feeling special. "You're welcome to dance with whomever you wish."

He couldn't be certain but she seemed somewhat disappointed in his answer before turning to the gentleman who'd made the offer. "Well, then, Lord Greyling, I'd be most delighted to take a turn about the floor with you."

"You must call me Grey," Marsden heard him say as he led her away. He didn't like how close they were, how Greyling smiled at her as though she were his favorite person in the entire world.

"You can't be thinking to marry her," Ashebury said once the couple had moved beyond hearing. "She'd never be accepted among the *ton*. Even now you don't see anyone rushing over for an introduction."

"I'm well aware she'd be ostracized." His title came with some influence, but the nobility liked to keep their ranks pure. Parentage mattered. "She's moving to London; has always wanted to attend an infamous Havisham ball. My Christmas and parting gift to her."

"Lady Marsden must have been thrilled."

Watching as Linnie waltzed with Grey, he did wish she weren't smiling so brightly, even as he was grateful she was having such a jolly good time. He wasn't so selfish as to wish her miserable when she wasn't in his company. "I promised Mother I would decide whom I would marry if she invited Linnie."

"Any contenders?"

"Not at the moment."

Ashebury shifted his stance. "Then stay clear of Lady Penelope Withers."

Marsden laughed at the quietly given but rather firm order. "You indicated you hadn't taken a fancy to anyone."

"I don't want Grey to get a whiff of my interest. His competitive nature will have him striving to win her over."

"You're a duke. Your title gives you an advantage."

"I don't want her marrying me for my bloody title."

While it was a challenge to turn his attention away from Linnie, Marsden forced himself to face his friend. "You can't mean to imply that you're in love with her."

Ashebury shrugged as though the comment were of no consequence but the tautness in his jaw gave away that it mattered a great deal. "I noticed her during the Season, but I kept my distance as she intrigues me in a manner that is rather unsettling."

Unsettled. Yes, that was a good description for how Marsden had begun to feel whenever Linnie was around. No, it was more how he felt when she wasn't around. He was always calmer, more himself when he was with her. "If you want her, you should lay claim to her before someone else does."

"You're right, of course. I simply didn't want to be the first among us to get married."

"A rather stupid excuse to let someone who intrigues you slip away."

"You make a good point."

They stood in silence for long minutes. Marsden turned his attention back to the dance floor, but he couldn't see Linnie. Too many blasted people.

"You could make her your mistress," Ashebury said quietly.

Marsden snapped his head around. "I beg your pardon?"

"The barmaid. You could serve as her benefactor."

He had a good mind to punch Ashebury in the mouth. "She deserves better than that."

"You can't tell me that you don't have a care for her."

"I do, which is the very reason I wouldn't entertain the notion of taking advantage."

"Pity. It appears your cousin hasn't the same qualms." He jerked his head to the side.

Marsden spotted Robbie with Linnie, near the mirrored wall. The rage erupting through him escaped in a bellow as he charged through the crowd.

"Come on, give us a kiss."

Greyling had been escorting Linnie from the dance floor when Robbie St. John had happened by to claim the next dance and the earl had foolishly placed her in his keeping before she could object. Only the oaf hadn't wanted a dance as he'd asserted but instead had backed her up against the wall before slipping a sprig of mistletoe from his pocket and holding it above her head.

"I'd rather spit on you; now leave off," she said for the third time.

"You know what they say. If you don't kiss a bloke when you're under the mistletoe with him, you're destined to be an old maid."

"Then I'll be an old maid."

Her back was against the mirrored wall and one of his

beefy hands was wrapped around her arm. She didn't want to make a scene and embarrass Marsden by her presence, but it was happening anyway. And ruining her night in the process.

"People are watching," he said. "They expect you to play along. Other girls have."

"Other girls have no self-esteem apparently."

He narrowed his eyes. "Stupid tavern wench. I'll take more than a kiss before this night is done."

Her palm striking his cheek barely turned his head, only served to make his mouth split into a mean-looking grin. He leaned in. "I'm going to have fun with you later, but I can't walk off now without a kiss. My reputa—"

He was gone, slammed against the wall so hard that she felt it shake and was surprised the mirror didn't crack. Stepping aside, covering her mouth with her hand, she watched with a mixture of horror and joy as Marsden pummeled his fist into Robbie's face, not once but three times. Groaning, cradling his jaw, the brute slid to the floor.

"Get anywhere near her again, and I'll have you kicked out into the cold," Marsden said, his voice low and vibrating with fury.

"She ain't a lady."

Marsden balled up his fist. She placed her hand on his arm, standing her ground when he directed those anger-filled eyes her way. "He's three sheets to the wind. No harm was done."

He held her gaze for several heartbeats. Finally he

gave a brusque nod before looking about and signaling to two footmen. "Get him to his room. Lock him in so he can sleep this off." As the footmen hoisted up his cousin, Marsden released a shuddering breath. "I'm badly in need of a drink."

"So am I," she said quietly.

Plastering a false grin on his face, he turned to those who had gathered around. "Entertainment's over. Carry on."

"Sorry, old chap," Greyling offered. "He said he wanted to dance with her. If I'd known—"

"You should have known. He's an idiot. I'm taking Miss Connor for a stroll."

She'd just reached down, picked up the mistletoe sprig, and tucked it into her pocket when Marsden slipped his arm around hers and began leading her through the crowd far too quickly. "You can't be angry at Grey," she said.

His jaw tightened. "When a gentleman takes a woman onto the dance floor, he is responsible for her reputation and well-being. He shouldn't have abandoned you."

"He didn't. He was passing me off to the next chap who expressed an interest in dancing with me."

Stopping abruptly, he glared at her. "Did you want to dance with Robbie? Did you want to be cornered by him? Did you want to kiss him?"

"No, of course not. Why do you think I smacked him?"

"Then don't defend Grey."

With that they were off again, ascending the stairs with incredible haste, and it occurred to her that he was troubled by something more than his cousin's abhorrent behavior. "Are you upset that I danced with Grey?"

Reaching the landing, they left the room and started down a hallway. "You seemed to be enjoying yourself."

"I like dancing."

"I didn't think you'd ever danced."

"Not the way the fancy folk do, but I've danced at village festivals."

He came to a halt and faced her. "With whom?"

"With whomever asked. It was all in fun, George. That's what life is about. Having fun. Don't ruin tonight by being angry."

"Robbie could have hurt you."

"Not likely. Had he gotten any nearer, his tender area would have been introduced to my knee." His eyes widened; she shrugged. "It's one of the first things that the tavern owner teaches us when he hires us—how to handle a man who's up to no good."

He chuckled. "I would have liked to have seen that. I'm wishing now that I hadn't interfered."

"To be quite honest, I'm rather disappointed it didn't get that far."

Taking her hand, he threaded his fingers through hers, as he had when they were children. She preferred it to simply placing her hand on his arm. It somehow seemed more intimate although she did wish they weren't wearing gloves.

"The gallery is this way," he said, escorting her down the hallway, his stride not quite as long or quick, his shoulders more relaxed.

"It must have taken centuries to collect all the little baubles in this residence." Decorative tables, knickknacks, statuettes, flowers, and paintings were everywhere. She'd hate being the one who had to dust them all.

"I suppose. Never gave it much thought."

They went up a short set of steps and into a wide corridor that three drays side by side could move through. One side was a wall of portraits, the other a wall of windows. Couples stood looking out on the falling snow or slowly strolled from one end to the other. No doubt courtship at play in many cases.

"Regarding the promise you made to your mother," she began as they neared the first painting, an elegant woman sitting in a chair holding a babe while two boys stood on either side of her.

"Yes?"

"Don't bother with Lady Edith Kipwick."

"Why ever not?"

They wandered down to a vertical line of small portraits of various children. "Greyling has an interest in her."

He grinned. "How do you know that?"

"He was asking me how best to go about wooing her."

He chuckled low, but still a few people turned their heads toward them. "It seems my friends may very well marry before me. Ashebury also has an interest in a lady. I can't fathom that they would fall so quickly."

"Is there a better time of year for falling in love?"

He didn't reply. She didn't expect him to. He took two flutes from a passing footman and handed her one.

"I was thinking of something a bit stronger when you said you were in need of drink," she told him.

"As was I but we must be discreet in slipping away to my library."

"Is our presence here an effort to throw others off the scent?"

His green eyes twinkled. "Indeed."

They were halfway along the corridor when she asked, "Are you related to all these people?"

"In one way or another."

"Such a sour lot. Not a single one of them smiling."

"One does not smile for portraits."

"Why not?"

"It's a serious matter. You're leaving your likeness for future generations."

"I can well understand your medieval ancestors not smiling. They probably had rotting teeth but the more recent ones—they all look doomed. If I ever sit for a portrait, I'm going to smile so those who come after will know I was happy."

"Are you happy?"

"Of course." *I'm here with you*, she almost added, but a time would come very soon when she might never see him again.

"I should like to have a miniature of you."

She peered up at him. "That wouldn't be wise, George. It might make your wife jealous."

He nodded. "Yes, you're right, of course. Ghastly idea."

They'd reached the end of the room. He glanced around somewhat surreptitiously. "Step into the stairwell there and head down. I'll catch up."

"Are we about to do something wicked?"

He winked at her. "Very wicked indeed."

CHAPTER 5

He caught up with her at the bottom of the stairs, grabbed her hand, and began jaunting through a warren of hallways. Her laughter followed in their wake, and he knew he would forever hear it whenever he walked the corridors.

"How in the world do people not get lost in here?" she asked.

"You learn your way around, but the possibility of getting turned about does keep most guests from exploring on their own."

"So you think we won't get caught?"

He grinned at her. "Rather sure of it."

Finally, they reached the library. Normally a footman would be standing guard, ready to open the door for him but tonight they were all needed to assist with the guests in one manner or another. Closing the door behind them, he locked it.

"Why did you do that?" she asked.

"Because if someone is wandering around, I don't want

you to be caught alone in here with me. It would send your reputation to the devil."

"As though I care about my reputation." She glided over to the windows. "I don't know if I'd get any work done in here. I'd forever be looking out." She spun around. "Or reading. My God, where did you get all the books?"

They filled an abundance of shelves. "Bookshops. At least the ones I've added to the collection. Most were acquired by my ancestors. Some of the volumes are extremely rare."

"All books are rare." She approached a shelf. "We have the Bible and that's about it. Do you have any notion as to how fortunate you are? All these treasures. The books, the paintings, the statues, the artwork."

"They're not really mine, Linnie. I'm more temporary custodian than owner. That's the way it is in my world. You focus on the next generation and leaving them something of worth. Brandy?"

She smiled. "Yes, please."

He wanted that smile captured on canvas. But she was correct. It wouldn't do to be carrying around a miniature of her in his pocket. He would be as true a husband as possible to the woman he married. Unlike his father.

He walked over and poured the amber liquid into two snifters. When he turned around, it was to find her sitting on the floor before the hearth. "You can sit in a chair, Linnie."

"I wanted to be near the fire and nearer to you. The chairs put too much distance between us."

"I could move a sofa over."

She patted the floor beside her. "Here is fine."

He knelt. "You'll get your pretty gown dirty."

She laughed. "George, I suspect I could eat off your floor. Now sit, with your back against the chair so you're comfy."

She took a snifter from him and he settled in, not surprised when she patted his leg, nudging it as though she were hinting he should spread them. "I want to sit with my back to your chest like I did when we were children."

Except then his back was against a tree, they were sitting in grass, and his cock didn't get hard with the mere thought of her nearness. "Probably not a good idea."

"It's a lovely idea." Before he could object again, she'd worked her way between his legs and snuggled in against his chest. "Cheers, George."

She sipped, while he gulped a good portion and tried to focus on the flames dancing on the hearth rather than the feel of her rounded bottom pressed so intimately against him. Even with all the petticoats and material of her gown, he was acutely aware of her shape. Near his mouth the long nape of her neck tempted him. Her bared shoulders were a distraction.

"Do you know Lady Evangeline?" she asked quietly.

He'd greeted all the ladies as each had arrived during the past two days. Most he'd been introduced to before but a few were new to him. "Blonde, blue eyes, ruddy cheeks."

"That's the one. Greyling introduced me to her after our dance, before Robbie made his appearance. You should marry her."

He needed to marry someone and quickly so he had a woman to bed before he exploded just thinking about bedding her. He couldn't seem to tame the wild thoughts rioting through him that with a bit of vigilance and caution he could actually secrete her into his bedchamber. And that would be so wrong. She was in his care tonight; he was responsible for her. He couldn't ruin her when he knew he couldn't offer her a lifetime with him. "Why?"

"She has wide hips. She shouldn't have any trouble at all giving you four strapping sons."

"Four?"

Nodding, she wiggled against him until she was nearer when he'd thought it impossible for them to be any closer. "I see you with four boys. Two dark-haired and two blond. Rapscallions all."

"No daughters?"

"Perhaps. I just don't see them."

"You can gaze into the future, can you?"

"Just a premonition. I get them now and again. Do you remember when those gypsies passed through one summer?"

"Of course. They put on a show with their jugglers and knife throwers. My uncle forbade me to go because he believed they only wanted to pick our pockets."

"But when I came for you, you went with me."

He couldn't help himself. He trailed his gloved finger from the area above her elbow along her bare skin to the short sleeve of her gown. "You'd have thought me a coward, otherwise."

"I went back the next day. An old woman read my palm."

"Did she promise you a lifetime of happiness?"

"An eternity of it, actually, but even so, she said I wasn't long for this world."

He stilled, his finger ceased its stroking. He couldn't imagine a world without her in it. Yet she'd be leaving his world when she moved to London. Once he married, he'd have to avoid her. No more laughing with her, no more conversations. No secrets shared. No more confessions. No more doubts and fears given over into her keeping, knowing that with her all would be safe. "Why would she tell a little girl something stupid like that?"

"Because she had the sight; she wanted me to make the most of what time I had remaining to me."

"That's ridiculous, Linnie. She was a stupid old hag who knew nothing." He placed his hands on either side of her shoulders and turned her slightly so he could look into her blue eyes. "You can't have believed her."

"I don't know that it matters. I don't fear dying, George. I fear not living life to its fullest. I have strived to make the best of every day. So perhaps it's not such a bad thing to acknowledge that tomorrow is not a guarantee. It makes us appreciate what we have right now and to make the most of it."

At that moment, he had her. "If I'd known we were going to escape to this room, I'd have had a basket with your bread and some cheese waiting for us so we could have had a picnic in here."

"Ah, so that's how you do it in winter. Inside."

"Exactly, although I've never done it before."

"That's how you can court Lady Evangeline."

He pressed his lips to the curve where her neck met her shoulder. "I don't see myself courting her."

"You promised your mother you'd court someone."

"I promised I'd choose."

"If you don't court her, she's not likely to say yes."

Grinning, he shrugged. "But my promise is kept even if she says no."

"Your poor mother. You must be a trial as a son."

"I try."

Laughing, she settled back against him. "I like your house."

"You haven't even seen all of it."

"I don't suppose we can stay in here very long. They'll start missing you."

After removing his gloves, he trailed his finger along her spine, from her neck to where the material gathered partway down her back. "We can stay as long as you like."

It was peaceful here, with the fire crackling, sending off its warmth. He finished off his brandy in one long swallow, watched as she occasionally sipped on hers. One of the things he liked about her was that they didn't have to always converse. He could enjoy her company in the silence and not feel odd about it.

She set her empty glass aside.

"Would you care for some more?" he asked.

"No, I don't think so." She shifted her position slightly, her backside rubbing against him provocatively, and he bit back a groan as his cock immediately jumped to attention. He'd been having such great success keeping it reined in, and all it had taken was one little movement from her for him to lose complete control. She turned, presenting him with her profile as she raised her arm. Between her fingers, over her head, dangled a sprig of green. "Your cousin said if I don't kiss a fellow when I'm beneath the mistletoe, I'll end up an old maid."

He never thought he'd be grateful to his cousin for anything. "The day we met you announced that you'd never marry."

"I was a child then. Now I suppose if the right gent asked, I might change my mind."

"Well then, we can't risk turning the fates against you, can we?" Taking her hand, he began peeling off her glove.

"What are you doing?"

"You might decide, during the kiss, that you want to touch my cheek or run your fingers through my hair. It'll be more pleasant for us both if you're not wearing gloves." The pleasantness had already begun with the revealing of her skin, flawless except for a small scar near her littlest finger where she'd once burned it on the oven. Now, he pressed a kiss to it before taking her other hand and patiently removing the kidskin.

Placing his hands on her shoulders, he turned her a little bit more before taking her face between her palms and claiming her mouth as his.

It was just as wonderful as she remembered, if not more so. His velvety tongue swirling over hers, his arm coming around to support her shoulders as he eased her down to the floor, one of his legs coming to rest between hers. The gown was lovely but the material too thick and it had far too many petticoats. At that moment she was wishing that she was wearing her tavern frock. It was much less cumbersome. Not that George seemed to mind.

He was slowly, provocatively lapping at her mouth as though she were a tasty treat and he could never have enough of her. His feral growl reverberated through his chest and into hers, inciting her desires. Not that much inciting was needed. She'd wanted him for far too long. She felt like a tinderbox that needed little more than a stray ember to send the entire thing into a conflagration.

He dragged his mouth along her throat and across her chin until he reached the soft skin below her ear. "We should return to the ballroom."

"Not yet," she whispered. "Please, not yet."

Lifting his head, he held her gaze. She loved how tormented, how conflicted, he appeared. He was a man of honor but also one who desired her.

"You tempt me, Linnie, you tempt me to do things I shouldn't."

"What do you want to do, George?"

"Devour you. From head to toe."

"Then devour. I shan't object."

"You should."

"But I shan't." She required neither reputation nor purity. She craved only memories of him that she could lock away in her heart to be viewed when they were no longer together.

"Merely a taste then." He lowered his head to the valley

between her breasts, dipped his tongue between the aching orbs. Then he trailed his lips over one swell, before journeying back to take the same path over the other. So gentle, so sweet, so forbidden.

Her nipples, more sensitive than usual, straining against the cloth, hardened and pearled, longed for what they were being denied. He closed his mouth around one turgid peak, the velvet no barrier to his heat. She cried out, arching her hips, shifting, pressing the core of her womanhood to his firm thigh, made strong by all the riding he did.

It wasn't enough. Although she'd never been with a man before, she knew there was more, that she should feel more. Tugging on his hair, she pulled his head back, rose up and took his mouth. Pushing herself up, keeping her mouth latched to his, she rolled him over until he was on his back and she could straddle him, her skirts and petticoats gathered around them, but no longer forming a barricade to what she wanted. Through his trousers she could feel the hard length of him straining against her thin undergarments, seeking the dampest part of her.

"Christ, Linnie," he groaned. "You don't know what you're doing to me."

"I know exactly what I'm doing. I want you, George. I want to feel you inside me."

"Jesus."

He slammed his eyes closed, but she wasn't having it. She tore at his cravat, untying the intricate knot, casting it aside until she could reach his neck and suckle on the soft skin, nipping at it with her teeth. "Unfasten me."

"This is madness."

"I'll go mad if you don't."

He released a short burst of laughter before threading his fingers through her hair and bringing her mouth back to his. So greedy, so determined, so skillful. He explored every valley, every rise. Taking her so deeply into the vortex of pleasure that she was barely aware of the tug on her lacings. Then her gown and corset loosened. And she was free. Free to breathe deeply, free to gasp, free to push herself up and shove the various layers of material down or move them aside, until her torso was bared.

His emerald eyes as he stared at her were more heated than the fire. He shoved himself up, bent his head, and swirled his tongue over her nipple before drawing it into his mouth, suckling hard, then gently before circling once again.

Closing her eyes, she dropped her head back. The sensations eddying through her were incredible. They came in undulating waves along her limbs, from fingertips to toes. Glorious. Smoldering. Retreating before growing in intensity.

She unbuttoned his waistcoat and shirt. Placing her hands beneath the parted material, taking delight in his sharp intake of breath, she slowly caressed his ribs, before moving the silk and linen aside to tease his nipple as he'd teased hers. "I knew you'd be beautiful," she whispered.

"Not as beautiful as you." He skimmed his hands up her back, his fingers dancing along her spine as he flattened his chest to her breasts and once again claimed her mouth.

Gliding his hand down her side until he reached her hips, he maneuvered her until she was once again lying with her back on the floor. She was keenly aware of his hand traveling up her leg, circling her knees.

He grinned devilishly. "Not so knobby." Holding her gaze, he took his hand higher. "Tell me to stop."

"No."

She watched his throat muscles work as he swallowed. His hand reached the apex at her thighs, his fingers parted the folds.

"You're so damned wet." He lowered his head. "And hot." He kissed one corner of her mouth, then stroked his tongue over her lips as his fingers caressed other lips. He thrust his tongue into her mouth as his fingers entered her lower. His thumb circled the swollen nubbin, toying with it as pressure built. He slid his mouth downward, taking her nipple between his teeth, tugging.

She whimpered as sensations spiraled. His fingers slid in and out, slowly, gently, his thumb swirled deliciously, pressing more firmly, insisting, insisting—

Everything within her exploded into a thousand stars, hurtling through the heavens. Before she could fully give in to the cry that burst up from the very core of her being, he'd covered her mouth with his, absorbing her scream, holding her close as her body jerked and spasmed with the force of the pleasure that ricocheted through her.

Only when she stilled did he release his hold. Draped over his lap like some limp rag doll, panting, with her nerve endings still tingling, she stared up at him. His expression was so soft and tender that she wanted to weep. "My word."

He grazed his fingers over her cheek, watched the movement. "The harm in a kiss. Sometimes it's difficult to stop."

"But you did stop." Having seen horses and dogs mating, she understood that he hadn't gone as far as he could have. "You didn't see to your own pleasures."

"I'm not going to take your virginity on the floor."

"We could move to a sofa."

Chuckling, he lowered his head and brushed his lips over hers. "Is it any wonder I adore you?"

Adore was not love but it was awfully close. "Does that mean we're moving?"

Sadly, he shook his head. "I won't ruin you, Linnie. I care for you too much to do that."

He wouldn't ruin her because he couldn't offer her marriage. It hurt. Even as she understood her place in his world, it hurt. "I should return home now."

He studied her for a long minute and she knew that he understood more than her words. He understood that not only the magic of the night was ending, but that she was saying goodbye to their friendship. "The ball will go on for another couple of hours," he said quietly, and she heard the disappointment. Things between them were changing. They were no longer children who could ignore their places in the world.

"Without me, I'm afraid. I have to help my father bake bread in the morning." Every Christmas they distributed loaves among the less fortunate in the village.

"Will you at least give me one more dance?"

"I suppose that's not too much to ask."

But first they had to set each other to rights. She didn't want to consider how personal it seemed, how it made her feel as though they were a couple taking care of each other. Even though he'd assisted her and assured her that every hair was in place, she feared that people would be able to discern that she wasn't quite as tidy as she'd been when she arrived.

He slipped his hand into hers and she rather wished they hadn't bothered to put their gloves back on. After unlocking and opening the door, he poked his head into the hallway before announcing, "All clear."

Once they'd left the room, he said, "We'll go back the way we came. Much less likely to be thought having participated in something untoward."

"Why is it considered wrong when it feels so lovely?" she asked.

"It's only wrong if it's done out of wedlock."

"Only if a lady does it out of wedlock. You fellows can have it as often as you like whenever you like with whomever you like and no one criticizes you."

"True, although I wouldn't say that to just anyone. Such talk could create quite the scandal."

"I think it might be fun to create scandal."

"Easy enough to say until you're the object of it." She knew he was thinking about his father and how his actions had brought scandal to the family. She'd been too young to understand when she was a child, but whispers of his death in a tavern maid's bed still surfaced from time to time. Little wonder his mother despised her.

When they reached the back stairs that led into the gallery, he stopped, brought her hand to his lips. She felt the warmth of his kiss through her glove. "I'll go up first. Count to twenty, then follow. If I determine our absence has been noted, I'll go on ahead. If you don't see me, carry on to the ballroom. Coming in separately should dispense any rumors."

His plan made her dizzy. So many games played in his world. Still she nodded and watched him go.

They made it to the ballroom without anyone the wiser regarding their absence. He was grateful to once again have her in his arms as they circled the dance floor. In the library, it had cost him to stop. He'd no doubt be aching all night. He wanted her. No, it was more than that. He needed her.

However, Ashebury was correct. Even in the gallery, he'd seen people observing her as though she were a curiosity, yet no one approached, no one asked for an introduction. It would be worse in London. If her father were a landowner or possessed wealth, it might be different. But he was the village baker and she was the baker's daughter.

When the dance came to an end, she gave him a sad smile. "It's nearly midnight, time to return to reality. I'd like to say goodbye to your mother."

Of course she would. While his mother's behavior toward Linnie might be abhorrent, his friend was not one to be ugly in return. He didn't know if he'd ever met anyone with a disposition as kind as hers.

They found the marchioness engaged in conversation with Greyling's and Ashebury's mothers, no doubt plotting their next scheme for getting their sons married. His mother moved away from her friends to greet them. Or admonish them. Her mouth was set in a hard line, her eyes flinty.

"You were gone from the ballroom for a while," she pointed out.

"We went for a stroll, as many of the couples are doing," he told her.

"Based upon how long you were gone you must have shown her the entire residence."

"Hardly."

As though sensing the building of tension, Linnie said, "I want to thank you for the lovely evening, Lady Marsden. I suspect it shall always remain one of my favorite memories."

"I'm glad you found the night to your liking."

"I found it interesting. I do hope your son's marriage will bring you happiness."

His mother's gaze snapped to his. "Have you decided?"

"Not yet. Tomorrow perhaps. Now I'm going to see Miss Connor home."

"Surely the maid you borrowed earlier can see to that."

"She'll be riding along, but I shall serve as escort as well. There could be highwaymen lurking about."

His mother scowled. "Not on the road between here and the village."

"Still, I'd best make sure. I won't be long."

He led Linnie out of the ballroom, retrieved her wrap, and located the maid. When they were settled in the coach, his dearest friend in the entire world said, "I really did have a lovely time, George."

The coach turned onto the main road. There was no lantern lit this time. The moon coming in through the windows provided just enough light that Linnie could see Marsden's silhouette as he reached up and banged twice on the ceiling. The driver pulled the vehicle to a stop. A footman opened the door.

"M'lord?"

"Sarah is going to ride up top to the village. Keep her warm."

"Yes, m'lord."

Without a word, Sarah scampered out and the door closed.

"What are you doing?" Linnie asked.

"I want to be alone with you." He moved over to her bench, took her in his arms, and kissed her.

As the coach began an extremely slow journey, she melted against Marsden, reached up, and threaded her fingers through his hair. He drew her onto his lap, angled her head slightly, and took the kiss deeper. Eventually he pulled back.

"I shall never be able to walk through Havisham without seeing you there."

She couldn't stop her triumphant smile. "Good. I want to haunt you."

"Oh, you haunt me, Linnie, in ways you can't imagine."

"Do you think we'd be friends if you were the blacksmith's son?" she asked.

"I should think so."

"Would we be more?"

He looked away. "I don't know. It wouldn't be a very fancy life."

"I don't need fancy. I also need to give this back to you." She unlatched the necklace and held it out to him.

"Keep it. Please."

She shook her head. "I can't." Taking his hand, she dropped the emerald and chain into his palm and closed his fingers around it.

He studied his fist as though it contained some dark secret. "My mother would never accept you."

"I know."

"Society . . . they didn't exactly welcome you tonight."

She pressed a kiss to his jaw. "I don't need them. I had you. That was enough."

"I wish I was the blacksmith's son."

"I don't." She kissed one corner of his mouth. "You are who you are supposed to be: my dearest friend. And that's enough."

With a groan, he blanketed her mouth. This, she thought, would be their last kiss. She would make the most of it. So she returned it with equal fervor and enthusiasm, absorbing his strength, his warmth, the scent that was unique to him. So much she loved about him, so much she would miss. But it was time to put away childish dreams.

The coach had been moving so slowly that it took her a moment to realize that it had stopped completely. Drawing back, he skimmed his fingers over her cheek. "Happy Christmas, Linnie."

"Happy Christmas, George."

He slid her off his lap, moved back across to his bench, and tapped the roof. The door immediately opened. He stepped out, then handed her down. She wasn't surprised to see her father standing in the doorway of the shop, his arms crossed over his chest.

She started to walk away, then stopped. "Whoever you choose, George, she will be a very lucky lady indeed."

Then she skirted past her father and entered the shop. She heard the door close.

"Are you all right?" her father asked.

With a nod, she headed for the back of the shop and the stairs that would lead to her bedchamber, halfway wishing that Father Christmas was real and would bring her what she truly wanted for Christmas: an eternity spent with the Marquess of Marsden.

CHAPTER 6

Linnie loved the smell of freshly baked bread, found it comforting, especially on Christmas. Once she'd put away the ball gown, she'd discovered it was difficult to sleep, holding all of the wonderful moments close, reliving them, knowing they would stay with her forever. Still, she had tossed and turned much of the night, wondering if Marsden had made his choice. She had little doubt that he'd returned to the ball to dance and flirt into the wee hours of the morning. He was probably still at it when she crawled out of bed at four to begin helping her father with the baking.

In addition to the bread, she'd prepared a large caldron of stew that she was now ladling into crocks that she would distribute to those who might otherwise go hungry this day. Giving to others was one of her favorite things to do.

The rap on the back door to the kitchens had her glancing over at her father. He merely shrugged and shook his head before returning to his task of removing the last of the golden-brown loaves from the oven. It was nearly seven so it was quite possible that a villager was anxious to claim some bread. They'd been gifting bread to those in need for as long as she could remember. Some had come to expect it.

But when she opened the door, she was surprised to find Marsden standing there. Surprised and glad. She shouldn't be so happy to see him, not when there could never be more between them than a friendship, not when she wanted more, not when it was quite possible that he'd adhered to his mother's wishes and made a decision regarding whom he would take to wife. Perhaps that was the reason he was here now, to tell her of his selection, to ask for her opinion. "What are you doing here?"

"It's snowing. I thought you might welcome the use of my coaches for making your deliveries."

Glancing past him, she saw three carriages lined up. The snowfall was light, nothing she hadn't trudged through before. "I'm not sugar, George. I won't melt if I get a bit wet."

"Do you really want to deliver soggy bread?"

No, she supposed she didn't.

"Besides, with my carriages, you'll also get my assistance so you can finish a bit earlier."

"What about your guests?"

"They'll be abed until noon at least."

She couldn't imagine sleeping most of the day away. "All right, then. Come on, give us a hand."

Most of Marsden's favorite memories involved Linnie. As the coach traveled slowly along the road, it was difficult to acknowledge that very few of his future ones would include her.

She sat across from him now with baskets of bread stacked on either side of her, while boxes of covered tins and crocks wedged him in. After taking her home the evening before, he'd returned to Havisham to dance and visit with the ladies listed on parchment in his mother's precise script. He'd invited each one to accompany him this morning for his annual pilgrimage with Linnie to see to the needs of those without. To a one they'd all declined.

"Did you get much sleep?" he asked her now.

"A couple of hours. I enjoy Christmas too much to spend it in oblivion. I'll sleep in tomorrow."

He doubted that.

"What of you?" she asked. "What did you do after you left me?"

"Danced a bit. Drank a bit more. Lost at cards. Won at billiards."

She glanced out the window at the open countryside. They were heading to some houses on the outskirts of the village. "Did you make your mother happy?"

"I'm beginning to think she is happiest when she is unhappy."

Smiling, Linnie shifted her gaze over to him. "Does that mean you didn't choose a woman to court?"

"Not yet. Not from among those on her list anyway. They bored me."

"Were you trying, George? Did you give them a fair shake?"

How like her to worry about someone else, the fairness of their life. "I was quite open-minded."

"Did you want to discuss any of them with me?"

"No, I don't think any of them will suit."

"Pity. I don't want you to get lonely when I leave."

His chest tightened and it felt as though his throat was striving to knot up. "When are you leaving?"

Lifting a delicate shoulder, she sighed. "Probably not for another year. I don't yet have enough money to see me through for the hard times. I know success won't come straightaway. My father has never been shy about sharing the struggles of owning a business. But I welcome the challenge of it."

Of course she did. She was the most optimistic and courageous person he knew. "Do you fear failing?"

"No. I fear never giving it a go. Failure at least means one tried, doesn't it?"

He held her gaze. "I asked a pointless question. You won't fail. I believe that with all my heart."

"Your belief in me means the world to me, George."

He wanted to give her so much more than his unconditional belief in her. He wanted to be the one to give her the world. Not that she'd take it. She wanted to earn it for herself.

The coach came to a stop. Linnie moved up to the edge of her seat. "Grab two of the tins, will you, George? Mrs. Wilkins lost her oldest boy to a fever a couple of weeks ago. I doubt she'll be up to cooking a holiday dinner for the family."

By the time their visit was over, Mrs. Wilkins wasn't

even going to be warming the stew that Linnie had brought for her. Instead she and her family would be joining the Connors for a meal at four that afternoon. By the time the last of the bread and crocks had been given out, George reckoned there would be nearly twenty people gathered around Linnie's table for a meal that afternoon—which meant when she returned home she'd begin preparing a meal for her guests.

Today wasn't the first time that he'd gone on the charitable rounds with her, but it was the first time he'd noticed how beloved she was, how kind and generous she was to others. She knew everything about everyone: who'd been ill, who'd suffered loss, who was to marry, who would soon be giving birth.

She truly cared about these people in a way his mother never had, in a way that he wanted his future wife to care. He wanted a partner who was interested in more than gossip, balls, and the latest fashions.

When they finally arrived back at the shop, he was weary but she appeared more invigorated.

"Thank you for coming with me, George," she said as he handed her down.

"I don't know where you get your energy."

"Helping others always revitalizes me." Rising up on her toes, she brushed a quick kiss over his cheek. "Enjoy the rest of your day."

Then she was bouncing toward the door.

"Will you be coming out with the carolers tonight?" he

called after her. A group from the village always came to the manor on Christmas.

She spun around. "Of course. Perhaps this year, you'll sing with us."

"You've heard me sing. I'm atrocious. If any of the ladies in attendance heard me perform they'd turn down my suit, without question."

She laughed, but there was a sadness in her eyes. "Then they don't deserve you."

Before he could respond, she'd disappeared into the house. But perhaps she had the right of it. Did any woman deserve to be married to a man who would always love someone else?

CHAPTER 7

Marsden heard the carolers, voices lifted in song, long before they actually arrived. Every year they strolled up the road from the village, regardless of the weather. This night, the snow continued to fall occasionally but the chilled winds whipped over the moors relentlessly. Most of their guests were still in residence, having enjoyed an abundance of goose and trimmings earlier in the evening.

Various games were being played in assorted parlors, but he'd been waiting in the front room, sipping his scotch, reflecting on the conclusion he'd drawn regarding the woman he wanted to marry. After returning home from his morning excursion with Linnie, he'd given additional attention to each of the ladies on the list his mother had provided. Exceptional candidates all. Lovely, demure, with a lineage that would do his heir proud. He'd spent the afternoon listening as each entertained with the piano-forte. He made time to get each alone—or as alone as possible with chaperones hovering—for a bit of conversation.

By the time the sun had set, he'd made his decision. He knew without a doubt whom he wanted for a wife. He'd already spoken with her father, gained his permission to ask for her hand. Was determined to do so before the night was done. He was not generally struck with nerves, but he knew it was quite likely she would turn him down.

As the carolers' voices became louder, he spied them approaching, downed the last of his scotch, and set aside his glass. He'd always looked forward to this moment on Christmas. As a lad, he'd wanted to join them, but his mother had always forbidden it. Not proper to mingle with those beneath them. Yet he found the villagers more fascinating than he found those in his social sphere.

As he headed into the foyer, the guests began pouring from the other rooms, no doubt drawn to the siren chorus of "Silent Night." When he spotted his mother, he opened the door and waited as she led the women out. Most stood beneath the portico to shield themselves from the gently falling snow. Once it was obvious that some were going to stay indoors, he excused himself and eased his way through the ladies, edging past the tight gathering until he reached the steps and was able to quickly descend. He heard some footfalls behind him. Apparently he wasn't the only one not adverse to a little snow. His actions seemed to spur others to venture out a bit more.

By the time he was standing in front of the carolers, there was a nice gathering of his guests behind him. He was aware of Ashebury and Greyling on either side of him, the ladies they'd taken an interest in clinging to their arms, no doubt seeking some warmth. As for himself, he didn't feel the cold. All his attention was on Linnie, third caroler from the right on the front row. Her father was two rows behind her, a head taller than the woman standing in front of him. In all, there were probably fifteen to twenty carolers, some holding lanterns.

Only a heartbeat of silence filled the air before "Hark! The Herald Angels Sing" floated around them. It was silly to imagine he could distinguish Linnie's voice from the others, and yet he could have sworn his ears were attuned to her. He even imagined her fragrance reached him, when that was impossible as the cold dulled so many senses, but it sharpened his vision as he thought she'd never looked lovelier. She held his gaze, and he felt as though she were saying farewell.

When the group was finished, they all stood smiling, but none as brightly as she. She could outshine all the stars in the heavens.

Their guests clapped politely. His mother stepped forward. "That was lovely. The servants shall be out shortly with some warm cocoa to take the chill off before you head back to the village."

"We'll have carriages readied to take you back," he said.

"We don't have enough," his mother pointed out.

"I'm certain our guests won't mind lending theirs, but first I have a gift for Miss Connor."

Linnie's eyes widened. "Now?"

"I can think of no better time." He stepped nearer to her. "Actually, I have two gifts for you, but you must choose which one you want."

"George—" She cleared her throat. "M'lord, you gifted me with an invitation to the ball, which I enjoyed a great deal. Nothing else is needed."

"Gifts are not necessarily about need, Miss Connor. But rather desire. The desire to give, the desire to receive." He reached into his pocket and pulled out a narrow, slender box. "Please."

She glanced around, and he knew she was uncomfortable with everyone staring at her. He was even aware of a few of his guests—the ladies in particular—easing forward for a better view. Linnie opened the box and stared down at the iron. "It's a key."

"To a shop in London," he told her.

Her brow furrowed, she looked up at him. "Whereabouts?"

"At the moment, I'm not exactly sure. It's more symbolic than the actual key. I thought in the new year, we could go to London and scout out exactly what you're searching for."

"You can't give me a shop."

"I shall front the money for it. When your bakery is successful, you may repay the loan."

She narrowed her eyes at him. "And the interest?"

She would make an excellent proprietor. "None. Just one friend helping another."

"They say lending money is the quickest way to ruin a friendship."

"Then we shall prove the exception. You know you want it, Linnie. Don't be stubborn."

Her suspicions easing, she smiled brightly and nodded.

"It'll be a while before I can do it on my own. You're very generous, m'lord. I thank you for the kind offer. I accept."

"Without seeing the other?"

"To own a shop in London has always been my dream. I don't need to see the other. You can't do better than this."

"Are you sure?"

"Quite."

He'd expected as much, but still he'd hoped she had other dreams, other desires. Perhaps she did but she thought them unattainable.

"Never settle on one thing without knowing all your options, daughter," her father said quietly.

She looked at him, before returning her attention to Marsden. "I don't see that it can be anything I'd want more than this and people are getting cold. Can we make it quick?"

He removed a small square leather box from his coat pocket. She stared at it as though he were offering her a snake. He shook his hand. "Open it."

She glanced around, before handing the key off to her father. Gingerly, she took the box and slowly lifted the lid. The lady beside her raised her lantern so Linnie could more easily see the ring of diamond and emeralds. Or perhaps the woman wanted a better view for herself.

Linnie closed the box and looked at him sadly. "George, I've told you that I can't accept jewelry from you. It's not appropriate."

"I know it's not. Unless . . ." He went down on one knee and took her hand. "I love you, Miss Connor. I always have. Will you honor me by becoming my wife?"

The marchioness's hoarse croak nearly drowned out Linnie's surprised gasp. "George William St. John, have you gone mad?" his mother shrieked.

"Probably." He held Linnie's gaze. "As I can't imagine she'd choose me over her dream of owning a bakery in London."

"Honestly, George," Linnie said, smiling, tears welling in her eyes, catching the lantern light, "you've always had such a dismal imagination. I love you so much, you dolt! Yes, I'll marry you."

Rising, with a shout of joy, he took her in his arms, swung her around once, and then planted his lips on hers. He heard some claps and cheers in the distance, but mostly he just heard Linnie's sweet sigh.

He wanted to take the kiss deeper, but that was for later when they were alone. Drawing back, he held her close while he waved a hand toward the manor. "Everyone, inside for some spirits and merriment."

"You can't be inviting the villagers inside—through the front door," his mother said.

"They're Linnie's friends. They'll always be welcomed at Havisham."

His mother sounded as though she were drowning. He was rather certain she was going to need her smelling salts before the night was done.

"You promised to choose one of the ladies from my list," the marchioness said, her voice seething with betrayal.

"I promised to consider them, which I did. They bored me. Not once did any of them make me laugh. None were willing to give up their warm bed to ensure that those in need didn't go hungry on Christmas. You wanted me to choose someone based on the circumstances of her birth. I wanted someone who didn't judge me on the circumstances of mine."

"She'll never be accepted by Society."

"In all honesty, Mother, I care not. I want to be what you and my father never were. Happy. And Linnie has always made me happy."

With that his mother harrumphed and marched into the residence.

"Are you sure about this, George?" Linnie asked.

He smiled at her. "I've been sure since I was twelve years old."

"You could have said something to me earlier."

"The day I met you, you declared rather convincingly that you'd never marry. Through the years, you never changed your tune on that."

"Because I always thought you beyond reach."

"Yet here I am, close enough to touch."

After glancing around, she returned her gaze to his, looked deeply into his eyes. "Now that we're alone, could we have a proper kiss, do you think?" she asked.

As the snow floated around them, he lowered his mouth to hers.

They were married in the spring, in the church in the village. All of the villagers and perhaps a dozen of the nobility attended the ceremony. Linnie's father had escorted her down the aisle to the altar where her handsome betrothed waited for her. Lady Marsden had sat unsmiling in the first pew. Linnie was determined to win her over, although since Marsden had moved his mother to a dower house in London, they wouldn't be spending that much time together. Already the marchioness was on her way there, having left shortly after the breakfast celebration following the exchange of vows.

In all honesty, Linnie was rather glad. Tonight was her wedding night, and she was grateful to have the residence to herself and Marsden. They'd spent the late afternoon and early evening touring the rooms, kissing in every one. Now wearing a diaphanous white nightdress, she waited for him in her bedchamber. He'd purchased her a new wardrobe that included silk undergarments. She couldn't quite get used to the fact that she was the lady of this grand residence, now a marchioness. Her father wasn't quite comfortable with her elevated position, but he wanted her to be happy. She knew that with Marsden she would be.

The door that separated his bedchamber from hers opened. He wore a silk dressing gown, a narrow V revealing a portion of his chest, a chest she would soon be running her fingers over. She shifted her stance, suddenly wondering if she should have waited for him in the bed instead of standing beside it.

"You didn't bother with slippers?" he asked.

"I didn't want you to have to waste time taking them off."

"This is a drafty old place, Linnie. You have to keep yourself warm."

"That's your job, to keep me warm. Now get to it."

Laughing, he took her in his arms and gave her a kiss that heated her to the core. They'd managed to sneak in a thousand kisses before today. Each one left her anticipating her wedding night. She wouldn't have objected if it had come early, but he was so blasted worried about her reputation, about not ruining her, about ensuring she was respected as she deserved.

"I have wanted you so badly for so long," he whispered near her ear.

"You've shown remarkable restraint."

"You've no idea." Leaning back, he held her gaze. "The first time, might be rather quick."

"It can be clumsy and awkward as well and I won't care. I just want to be with you. I have for the longest."

Without taking his gaze from hers, he began unfastening her buttons. Reaching out, she untied his sash. The material parted and she was viewing considerably more than his chest. "My word."

He grinned. "Hopefully you'll be saying *that* a good deal tonight." He slid her gown off her shoulders. It slithered along her body, pooled at her feet. "Dear God."

She smiled bashfully. "Hopefully you'll be saying *that* quite often tonight."

"You are so beautiful, Linnie. Not a knobby knee in sight." He shrugged off his dressing gown, lifted her into his arms, and carried her to the bed. When he tossed her onto the mattress, she laughed, welcoming him with open arms as he followed her down.

He stole her laughter with a thorough kissing that caused every aspect of her body to curl. He was as hungry for her as she was for him. On some level, she thought she should be more demure, but this was George. They knew everything about each other, everything except for this.

But she was learning so quickly the feel of the hair on his legs as she ran the sole of her foot along his calf. The firmness of the muscles along his back as she scraped her fingers up them, the way they quivered when he moved. The eager thrusting of his tongue as he deepened the kiss, as he left no part of her mouth untouched. The roundness of his buttocks as she cupped her hands over each firm cheek. The way he growled and groaned. The enticing manner in which his breathing hitched.

The way he slid his mouth from hers and closed it around one nipple as his hand kneaded her breast, sending warm shivers cascading through every inch of her body. He made her feel delicate yet powerful. Her skin tingled with incredible sensations. How was it that even the places he hadn't yet touched seemed more alive, more aware, more sensitive?

He eased down, dotting kisses along each rib as he went, slowly lowering himself until he reached her navel, circling his tongue around it, looking at her with a smoldering hunger burning in his eyes. She plowed her fingers through his hair, closed her legs around his hips, squeezed. "You're making me feel marvelous," she whispered.

"You're going to feel even better."

He pushed himself down farther until he was blowing cool air across her curls. She wondered if she were a wanton because there was no part of herself that she didn't want him to see, to touch. She wished to share every aspect of her body with him.

"Do you ever touch yourself here?" he asked, his voice throaty.

Biting down on her lower lip, she nodded. "Sometimes when I think of you, late at night when I'm abed and all is quiet."

His grin was one of satisfaction and wickedness. "I stroke my cock when I think of you."

"Do you think of me when you're with other women?"

"There was only that one time I mentioned. To be quite honest, I wasn't doing a good deal of thinking."

"You said it went quickly. More quickly than this?"

"Much more quickly. I didn't take the time to explore her, to get to know her body, to learn what pleased her. But then I didn't love her. She wasn't the sort who required love, only coin. While it felt good, in the end, it left me wanting."

"I don't want to leave you wanting."

"You couldn't if you tried." Lowering his head, he stroked his tongue over the silken flesh.

Her eyes rolled back in her head; she released a languid sigh, which served to spur him on. He licked and suckled. Nipped and caressed. With his mouth, he worked wonderful magic, causing pleasure to riot through her. His fingers toyed with her nipples. She wrapped her hands around his wrists, because she needed something to anchor herself as it all became too much. Her thighs trembled, her hips strained to be nearer to him. She hovered on the edge of ecstasy. So close, so close . . .

Her cry echoed around them as pleasure ripped through her, hard, fast, intense. She was gasping for air, her body trembling uncontrollably. Before she'd fully returned from the summit, he'd slid up to hover over her and thrust his cock inside her. He stretched her, filled her. She was so enthralled by the feeling of him pounding into her that she barely noticed the slight discomfort. It was so brief. Then the marvelous sensations once again rippled through her as he rocked against her.

She skimmed her hands over his chest, his back, down to his buttocks. Back up and over. She couldn't get enough of touching him. She loved the way his hair flopped against his brow, the way he kept his gaze on her, the heat burning in his eyes.

"Scream for me again, Linnie," he rasped.

The pleasure took hold, undulated through her with each thrust. She was climbing, ascending. "Scream with me."

He moved faster, harder. She rocked her hips, in tandem with his movements. Her scream of release was quickly followed by his low growl as he arched back and jerked forcefully before going still, breathing harshly.

He lowered his face to the curve of her neck, placed a gentle kiss against her skin. "I love you."

"As well you should, m'lord."

Laughing, he rolled off her and brought her up against his side. "I was hoping to make it last all night for you."

She trailed her finger over his chest. "We can do it again, though, can't we?"

"Hmm, yes, but I need a moment to recover."

"I'm glad your mother wasn't here to hear me crying out."

"I like that you're so vocal in your enjoyment."

"Do you think ladies of quality make that much noise?"

"You're a lady of quality."

"I never want you to regret marrying me, George."

With his finger tucked beneath her chin, he tipped her face up until she was looking in his marvelous green eyes. "How could I ever regret marrying my dearest friend?"

"I think we're very fortunate to have each other."

"And now I'm ready to have you again."

She laughed as he went about doing just that.

CHAPTER 8

Christmas, 1851

Through the years, the Christmas Eve ball at Havisham Hall had become a much anticipated affair. Marsden had expected this year's to be cancelled as Linnie was nearing the time when she should go into seclusion before giving birth, but she had insisted she was up to the task of hosting the annual celebration. He was grateful for the opportunity to dance with her in his arms, even if he couldn't hold her as close as he'd have liked.

She was more beautiful than ever, her smile bright, her blue eyes twinkling. "Look merry, George."

"I am."

"No, you're worried. I told you that I'm feeling fine." She gave a quick grimace. "Except this son of yours is such a kicker. I fear he is going to be a handful, always getting into things. I don't think he's going to be very good at sitting still."

"I don't think that'll be a problem. He has all of Havisham through which he can roam."

"He's going to run through it. I sense it. What do you think of naming him Killian? It's a strong name, and I like it."

"Then we'll name him Killian, although I suspect he'll be addressed by his courtesy title more than anything. Viscount Locksley."

"Locksley is an awfully big name for a little one." Her smile turned sad. "I wish our parents were here to see him born."

Cancer had taken the marchioness two years after they married. A year later, Linnie's father had finished baking the day's bread and gone to take a nap. He never awoke.

"I'm certain they'll be looking down from heaven," he told her.

"I didn't think you believed in anything as whimsical as all that."

"I'll believe if doing so will return your smile."

"You spoil me, m'lord."

He tried. He loved her so much. More each day. His mother had been incorrect. The *ton* had come to accept Linnie, no doubt because of her generous heart and kindness. And she was just damned fun. She made him laugh, brought joy into his life, made him a better man.

The music stopped. Linnie took in a deep breath. "I must sit for a while."

He escorted her to a chair. He'd barely stepped back before two ladies rushed over to see how their hostess was faring. Yes, she was quite loved by the aristocracy.

He wandered through the room, carrying on small conversations here and there, making an introduction when one was needed. But he kept his attention focused on Linnie, wanted to be at her side in a wink if she signaled that she needed anything.

He ascended the stairs to the landing and gazed out over the ballroom. His mother would not have been pleased to see that it was more crowded than any ball she'd ever given. People loved experiencing the joy that circulated through Havisham now that a different marchioness was at the helm.

He was soon joined by Ashebury and Greyling, who handed him a tumbler of scotch.

"Up for billiards?" Ashebury asked.

"I don't want to wander that far from Linnie."

"You're worrying overmuch."

"Her time is near. We probably shouldn't have had this ball."

"Penny had the servants redoing the nursery the day before she gave birth," Ashebury said.

The ball where the Undecided Lords decided had turned out to be exactly that. Ashebury had married Lady Penelope six months later. Greyling had taken Lady Edith to wife a month after that.

"Took you so long to get her with child that I was beginning to wonder, old chap, if you knew what to do with that appendage dangling between your legs," Greyling said haughtily. "I already have my heir and my spare."

Marsden scoffed. "It's not such an accomplishment when your wife delivers them on the same day. And I'm only a year behind you."

"You're two years behind Ashebury."

He, too, had his heir. "I enjoyed having time alone with Linnie. Things change once a residence is filled with children."

"I suspect they'll change more for you than they did for us," Ashebury said. "I can't imagine your wife hiring a nanny."

"She likes to do things for herself."

"Still a commoner at heart then."

"Still the woman I love."

One Month Later

He didn't know what was worse: the two days of screaming or the sudden silence. He downed what remained of his scotch. He'd been downing it ever since Linnie went into labor, but it hadn't helped to numb his senses. If anything they seemed sharper than ever before. There was no place in this residence that he could go where he didn't hear her agony. Once he'd thought of trudging down into the mines that provided an income for Havisham, but he couldn't abandon her. In truth, he wanted to be at her side, but the physician was insistent that it would only make things harder for her because she'd worry about him. Yes, she worried about everyone except herself.

He leaped to his feet at the sound of rapid footsteps. Sarah Barnaby bolted into the room.

"It's a boy, m'lord," she announced.

The joy at having his heir speared him. Although to hell with Linnie's prediction that he'd have four sons. He was not going to let her get with babe again, was not going to have her suffer through this torment in order to provide him with even a spare. One child was all they needed, all he required.

"But something's terribly wrong, m'lord."

"With my son?"

"With her Ladyship. You'd best come quick, m'lord." Sarah burst into tears and sank into a chair.

Trepidation sliced through him, cold chills danced along his spine. He ran. Fast and hard, his heart pumping as quickly as his legs. He burst into Linnie's bedchamber. Chalky white, she lay in the bed, her damp hair plastered to her face. She gave him a weak smile. His knees were stiff as he began moving toward her. Suddenly the doctor, young and almost as pale as Linnie, was standing in front of him.

"I can't stop the bleeding, m'lord."

"Then what are you doing standing here? Get back over there and try."

He shook his head. "She's lost too much blood."

"Then you'd better damned well figure something out." Shoving him aside, he hurried over to the bed and sat down gently on its edge. "Hello, my love."

"Isn't he beautiful?" she whispered.

Only then did he notice the babe with a thatch of black hair, wrapped in swaddling, cradled in her arms. Tears burned his eyes. "He is indeed."

"You're going to have to love him for both of us."

Shaking his head, he lowered himself until he was certain that she could easily gaze into his eyes. "No, Linnie, you're not going anywhere."

"I was wrong about the four sons."

"One is enough. We'll be happy with one."

"I'm so tired, George."

Gently, he brushed back her hair. "You can sleep for a bit, but only for a bit. Then you'll start to get strong again."

She gave him a sad smile. "I fear the old gypsy was right."

"No. She was a stupid woman."

She shook her head. "I'm not long for this world, my love."

"Don't say that, Linnie. For God's sake, please don't leave me."

"I won't, George. I promise. I'll never leave you."

Only between one heartbeat and the next, she did.

CHAPTER 9

Marsden stood beside the grave where his beloved now slept. A month earlier, nobility and villagers alike had come to see her laid to rest. She was resting beneath the boughs of the great oak where he'd first met her. It was where she belonged. When his time came, he would lie beside her.

"Because you refused to bury her in hallowed ground," the vicar had told him, "her soul will find no peace."

But Marsden had known that she would have preferred being here, nearer to the grand house that had always fascinated her. And he imagined, although it seemed rather self-serving, that she would find peace in being nearer to him.

As for himself, he'd never known such profound grief and despair. He had the clocks in the residence stopped at the moment of her passing. He ordered that the servants touch none of the chambers in the residence. Whenever he walked into one of the rooms, he felt her there, envisioned her greeting him, inhaled her orange fragrance, heard her laughter, saw her smile. It was as though the very essence of her still occupied every corner and he didn't want to lose that lingering sensation that she was still with him.

He feared if he lost the minute details of her existence that he wouldn't be able to carry on.

Snow began falling, and he cursed it because it would send him indoors. Linnie would have waltzed through it, giggled as the flakes landed on her eyelashes and melted. He missed the joy she brought into the world. Missed her terribly.

It was nearly dark when he finally wandered back into the residence. A young footman stepped forward to take his coat and shake off the snow. "Shall I alert the cook that you're ready to dine, m'lord?" he asked.

"No, Gilbert, I have no appetite."

"With all due respect, sir, you need to keep up your strength."

"Why, when life no longer has any meaning?" He shuffled down the hallway, lacking the will to even lift his feet properly.

In the library, he sought meaning at the bottom of a bottle of scotch. He'd done it every night since her passing. It brought no comfort but at least ensured he slept, albeit fitfully. Until the sun again rose and he could return to her graveside.

It was past midnight when he stumbled upstairs. He was nearly to his bedchamber when he heard the small mewling coming from the nursery. His heart tightened. Sarah, serving as his son's nurse, slept in the room. She would see to the babe.

The residence went quiet. All he could hear was the shrieking of the wind beyond the walls. Since Linnie's passing, it seemed more grating, higher pitched. Or perhaps he only imagined that it mirrored the constant screams of sorrow echoing through his head.

He turned for his bedchamber, stopped. He'd seen the boy that afternoon. Suddenly he had a strong urge to visit with him again. He wouldn't be disturbing Sarah as she was no doubt already up, having done what was necessary to quiet him.

Only when he entered the nursery, he saw that the woman leaning over the bassinette, humming softly, wasn't Sarah. The nurse was sleeping soundly, snoring quietly, in the small bed in the corner of the room.

His heart lurched. Cautiously he approached the vision in white. He'd imagined seeing her in other rooms, but never quite this clearly. "Linnie?"

She smiled at him. "Don't look so surprised, George. I promised to never leave you."

He reached out to her, but there was nothing there. She was as substantial as mist, no doubt a figment of his inebriated mind.

"You're blaming our son, and it's not his fault," she said.

"I blame myself. If I'd kept my cock in my trousers—"

"What fun we'd have missed out on."

He couldn't deny those words. They'd made love in nearly every room. Save this one. The nursery seemed inappropriate.

"Don't become bitter with regrets, George. Celebrate what we had. Teach our son to love. See that he's happy."

He nodded. She was right. He needed to carry on. For Killian's sake. Killian St. John, Viscount Locksley. The precious heir she'd given him. "I miss you, Linnie, so damned much."

"I know, but I'm not so far away."

He glanced over at the sleeping Sarah. How was it that his speaking hadn't wakened her? When he looked back toward the bassinet, Linnie was no longer there, leaving him to wonder if she ever had been.

CHAPTER 10

November, 1858

The villagers believed him to be mad. Sitting at the desk in his library, he hardly blamed them, wondered himself at his sanity, because what sane man truly believed with all his heart and soul that his dead wife remained with him? What sane man would carry on conversations with her, seek her advice, tell her about his day? It was inconceivable, and yet he felt her presence so keenly, so strongly—especially out on the moors. Their son didn't see her, didn't sense her nearness but then he was only a child, even if he did seem to be growing up far too quickly. Killian, Viscount Locksley, was all of six now and such a precocious—

He jumped to his feet. "Locke! Get down from those shelves immediately!"

Rather than climb down from his perch halfway to the ceiling, he leaped. Marsden held his breath, waiting for the cry that would signal he'd broken his legs, but the fearless lad simply landed, bounced up to his feet, and didn't bother to look the least bit guilty even though he'd been chastised dozens of time for his penchant to scramble over the shelves like a wild monkey.

Marsden walked over to a shelf, pulled down a large book, and returned to his desk. "Come here."

Locke—Marsden couldn't seem to get into the habit of thinking of him as Killian. The shortened version of his courtesy title seemed more suited to him—wandered over, studying his father with what looked to be a bit of trepidation. The boy wasn't frightened of him, but he did seem to be cautious in all things, except for climbing.

Marsden patted his thigh. "Up you go."

The lad clambered onto his lap. He was a wiry boy, but not unhealthily so. Like his father, he'd no doubt be a slender man, not prone to acquiring a belly. All his activity no doubt taking its toll.

"Now." Marsden opened the book. "This is an atlas. It contains maps of many places in the world." He found the page he sought and pointed to a penciled drawing. "This is a mountain. *This* is what you climb. Not the shelves in our library."

The boy looked up at him with bright green eyes. "Where is it?"

"You'll find them all over the world. Even in Great Britain. This mark here"—he pointed on a map—"signals that a mountain is there. You can go through the book and find all the mountains. Then when you grow up, you can go off and climb them."

Locke's face broke into a wide grin. "Will you go with me?"

"No, lad, I must stay here, watch over things. That's what a marquess does."

"I don't want to be a marquess. Ever."

He ruffled his son's thick black hair. "Someday you won't have a choice, but until then, you can travel. I've taught you to read so you can start making your plans to be an intrepid explorer."

Locke turned his attention back to the book and began studying the drawings. Marsden doubted this task would keep him occupied for an hour, but if it kept him off the shelves for even a day, he'd be content.

He looked up at the soft footfall and watched as his butler approached, carrying a salver. He extended the silver tray. "A Mr. Beckwith has arrived, m'lord. He has three lads with him."

He took the card, glanced over it. Solicitor. Why would a solicitor bring him boys? As he rose to his feet, he managed to shift his son onto the chair. "Study the maps, Locke."

He strode from the room, into the hallway. When he reached the foyer, he saw the bespectacled man standing there, three young lads with worrisome expressions gathered around him as though he were a mother hen. The man snapped to attention.

"My lord, I'm Charles Beckwith, solicitor—"

"So your card said. Why are you here?"

"I brought the lads."

"What use have I for lads?"

Beckwith pulled back his shoulders. "I sent you a missive, my lord. The Duke of Ashebury, the Earl of Greyling, and their wives were tragically killed in a railway accident."

He'd seen the article in the *Times*. Had grieved their passing. He hated death and the loss it wrought. "Railway. If God meant for us to travel in such contraptions, He'd have not given us horses."

"Be that as it may," Beckwith said evenly, "I had expected to see you at the funeral."

"I don't attend funerals. They're ghastly depressing." And there was little he could do for them now. Besides, he was hesitant to leave Linnie. He feared if he left she might go away completely.

"Which is the reason I've brought the lads to you—since you didn't retrieve them yourself."

"Why bring them to me?"

"As I stated in my missive—"

"I don't recall a missive."

"Then I offer my apologies, my lord, for its being lost in the post. However, both the duke and earl named you as guardian of their sons."

Marsden homed his gaze in on the boys. He couldn't recall their exact ages, but he knew they were only a year or two older than Locke. The tallest had dark hair. The other two, the twins, were blond. They had so much growing up to do, so much to learn. Furrowing his brow, he gave his attention back to Beckwith. "Why would they be foolish enough to do that?"

They knew him to be in mourning; they'd barely communicated since Linnie passed.

"They obviously trusted you, my lord."

Marsden cackled. Had they not learned anything since the death of his wife? Had they not heard the rumors that Havisham was haunted, that he was mad?

The dark-haired lad rushed forward and punched his balled fist into Marsden's gut again and again. He packed quite a wallop.

"Don't you laugh," he shouted, tears filling his eyes. "Don't you dare laugh at my father!"

"Easy, lad," Beckwith said, pulling him back. "Nothing is accomplished with fisticuffs."

Breathing heavily, the child didn't look convinced.

"Sorry, boy," Marsden said. "I wasn't laughing at your father, merely the absurdity of my seeing to your care."

"But you will honor their request," Beckwith stated emphatically.

What the devil was he going to do with four boys?

I see you with four strapping sons.

The memory of those words was like a sharp kick to the center of his chest. Linnie could not have been referring to these boys. A woman with wide hips was supposed to give him sons. Not death.

But he knew in his heart that he would never again take a wife, that he would never again lie with another woman, that he wouldn't fill another with his seed. The reality was that Linnie had seen him with four sons. And the last of them had just been delivered. He gave a quick nod. "I will. For friendship's sake."

"Very good, my lord. If you could send some footmen out to retrieve the lads' trunks—"

"Have your driver and footman bring them in. Then be on your way."

Beckwith seemed to hesitate, but eventually he knelt before the boys. "Keep your chins up, be good lads, and make your parents proud." Then he stood and narrowed his eyes at Marsden. "I shall be checking on them."

"No need. They're in my care now. Be off with you as quickly as possible." He looked toward the windows. "Before it's too late."

With a slow nod, Beckwith turned on his heel and walked out. No one moved. No one spoke. The trunks were brought in. Shortly afterward, the creaking of the coach's wheels, the pounding of the horses' hooves signaled their departure.

"Locksley!" Marsden shouted, having noticed his son crouched behind some fronds. He should have known the boy wouldn't stay put in the library. His curiosity was too great.

"Yes, Father?"

"Show them upstairs. Let them select the bedchamber they want."

"Yes, sir."

"It'll be dark soon," he said, distractedly. "Don't go out at night."

Still reeling from the memory of Linnie's long ago words,

he wandered back into the shadowy hallway and into his library. He poured himself a glass of scotch, then he stood at the window, savoring the taste and waiting for the darkness. She never appeared during the day. For some reason, his mind wouldn't conjure her when the sun was out. It was more imaginative at night. Intellectually he knew she wasn't still here, that ghosts didn't exist—but damned if he didn't want to believe.

So he held his vigil until the sun disappeared over the horizon. He was about to step out on the terrace when the butler announced that dinner was ready to be served.

He always ate dinner with Locke. He certainly couldn't ignore their tradition tonight, especially when they had three newly minted orphans in residence. Speaking with Linnie would simply have to wait until later.

The young maid tasked with looking after Locke had seen that all the boys were properly presented for dinner. Marsden sat at the head of the table, sipping his wine, while plates were brought out. What a somber lot they were.

"Is the wind always so loud?" one of the blond-haired lads asked.

"Which one are you?" Marsden inquired.

"Edward."

"The heir?"

"No, that is I," the other blond said haughtily. As the rightful heir would.

"So, Edward," Marsden pointed, "Greyling and Ashebury and Locksley." He touched the center of his chest. "Marsden. Now we all know each other. And yes, the wind shrieks over the moors on more occasions than not but you'll get used to it."

"Did you really know our fathers?" Ashebury asked.

"I did indeed. We were best mates. As a matter of fact, your fathers met your mothers at a ball here. The ball where the Undecided Lords decided who they would wed. Then we all got busy with our wives and our children . . . and time went on."

"I don't want to be here," Edward said, mutiny in his voice. So he was going to be the one who required a firmer hand.

"There is much in life that we do not want, but we adjust." He glanced over at the butler. "Inform the cook: a double heaping of dessert for each of the boys tonight."

"You don't have many servants about," Ashebury said. "Are you poor?"

"Hardly. I don't need them, and I don't like having people around. Haven't decided yet if I'm keeping you lot."

"Send us home. We don't care," Edward declared.

"I can't do that. I'd have to send you to a workhouse. Horrid place that. So you'd best behave."

"I'm not afraid."

"I'd wager that makes you the only one at the table who isn't."

"Are you afraid?" Greyling asked.

"Of course I am. Afraid I'll let your fathers down. They were good men. I admired them very much. Someday I'll tell you stories about them."

"I want them to stay," Locke announced. "If you let them stay, I won't climb the shelves anymore."

"Did you think that was up for negotiation?"

Locke nodded, his hair flopping onto his brow. Chuckling, Marsden ruffled the dark strands. "You don't even know what negotiation means. Anyway, I suspect they'll be staying. For a while."

Following dinner, he handed them over to Sarah and then began his walk over the moors. The hairs on the nape of his neck rose, and he imagined that the boys were watching from a window. He was grateful when he was finally beyond their sight. He didn't need anyone to see him speaking as though to himself. He'd made the mistake of asking a few of the servants if they'd seen his wife wandering about. One of the reasons that he had only a handful of servants now was that few wanted to be associated with a madman.

So be it. His and Locke's needs were simple. The lads who had come to him today would have to adjust.

He reached the oak tree and stood before her grave. Her presence was strongest here. "Dear God, Linnie, you were right. I have four boys. Ashebury's and Greyling's sons."

"I know," she said. "They're afraid."

"They want to run off. At least one of them does. I'll have to keep a close watch until they realize they can't escape as they've nowhere else to go, no way to survive." He shook his head. "What am I going to do with four boys?"

"Love them."

"You were the one who was so good at loving."

"You'll be a good father to them. You understand the pain of loss, but they also need softness. They need a mother. It's time for you to move on, my love. To take another wife."

It wasn't the first time she'd urged him to marry. They'd argued about it on more than one occasion. "I will never love another. You own my heart. I saw what being unloved did to my mother. I would never ask another to suffer as she did."

"You would be kind to her and generous."

"But I would not love her and she would know it." He shook his head. "I haven't got it in me to be that cruel. The lads won't lack for a woman's touch. Sarah will spoil them well enough. I suspect Cook will slip them biscuits and sweets."

"You're a stubborn man, George."

"I adopted my wife's trait for stubbornness."

"You need to lock the doors and windows."

He furrowed his brow. "Why?"

"To keep me out."

"I like you coming into the residence."

"And I enjoy visiting with you there, but I don't want to frighten the lads. It'll be easier on me if I'm not tempted to go in."

"I miss you so damned much, Linnie."

"I'm here, George. I'm always here."

But he couldn't hold her or kiss her or make love to her. "Do you remember the rainy afternoon when we made love in the music room?"

She smiled. "On top of the piano."

"And beneath it. Sometimes I think that's my favorite day, but then I'll remember another. We had some good days, Linnie. And nights. I don't know if that makes being separated from you harder or easier." He sighed. "I don't know if I have it in me to raise these lads."

"You do. You're stronger than you realize."

"Only as long as I have you."

"You'll always have me."

CHAPTER 11

Christmas Day
1887

It's time, my love.

He awoke to the softly whispered words and the echo of ticking clocks.

With a sense of peace and contentment rolling through him, he threw aside the covers and climbed out of bed. For the first time in years, he wished he had a valet to see him properly groomed and dressed, but he'd make do. It had been a long while since he'd given such care to his appearance. He took a razor to his face and a brush to his hair.

He began donning his finest attire. He wanted everything perfect for her. He always had. Even if now he was bent and wrinkled, he could still dress sharply.

He thought he should have been frightened or wary, but all he felt was calm. And gladness. He was going to be with his Linnie again.

He walked out of his bedchamber and down the stairs

into the foyer. He glanced into the parlor at the decorated tree and the boughs of evergreen hanging along the mantel. This residence was indeed a happy place, perhaps even happier than it had ever been. All of his boys had fallen in love and married. Locke had been the last. He'd required a little nudging, which Marsden had provided. Portia was a remarkable woman, perfect for his heir. She'd given Locke a daughter and a son. They'd soon be tearing through the residence, wondering what Father Christmas had brought them. Later in the morning, one of the servants would be placing two crates, each holding a rambunctious puppy, beneath the tree. His family would find joy today, even if it was mixed with a bit of sorrow.

He strode out into the dawn. Snow was gently falling, but he didn't regret leaving his coat behind. He was immune to the chill, traveling a familiar path, one that had always brought him solace.

In the distance, he saw the towering oak, its branches spread wide. For a brief moment, in his mind, he saw himself as a boy sitting up there, a mischievous girl beside him. Within his chest, his heart thumped more forcefully than it ever had before. He stumbled, righted himself, and carried on.

He reached the graveside with its solitary marker. Without hesitation, he dropped to his knees, lowered himself to the ground, pressing one side of his face to the cold earth, his fingers touching the icy marble. "I'm here, Linnie. I'm here, my love."

Closing his eyes, he waited for what was to come.

He felt the tender touch on his cheek, gentle but firm, and the warmth spread throughout his body. Opening his eyes, he saw her crouched beside him, more vivid than she'd been since her death. Her blue eyes were sparkling, her smile bright. The gladness that swept through him would have brought him to his knees if he were standing. Pushing himself up so he was sitting, he cradled her cheek. Solid, warm, so real.

"You're as beautiful as you were on the day we wed," he said. "And I'm so old and wrinkled—"

"No, you're not. In my eyes, you never aged."

He noticed his hand then. The once gnarled and bent fingers were straight, the wrinkles absent. Only now did he notice that his aching bones no longer ached. He was as he'd once been.

Linnie arose and extended her hand. He placed his in it and shoved himself to his feet. She began to lead him away.

They'd taken perhaps a dozen steps, when he stopped. He could no longer stand it. He'd waited more than thirty-five years. She looked up at him with questioning eyes. He drew her close and lowered his lips to hers.

The sweetness of it, the warmth of her mouth opening to him nearly undid him. Memories assailed him of every kiss they'd ever shared. She still tasted of oranges. Smelled of them as well. He'd always loved that about her, but then he'd loved everything about her.

Pulling back slightly, he rested his forehead against hers. "How is this possible? You feel so real, so solid."

"You're with me now. Truly with me."

He'd known, of course, yet still he gazed over his shoulder to see his earthly form lying prone over her grave. No remorse, no regrets, no sadness touched him. He turned back to her. "I've missed you, Linnie."

"I never left you, George."

"I know, but we weren't together like this."

She cradled his cheek. "You should have remarried. Long ago."

Slowly he shook his head. "It was always you, Linnie. I know you worried about me being alone, but the years passed swiftly and I would wait through them all again for you. You alone bring me happiness."

"And now we shall have an eternity of it," she said softly.

Placing her hand in his, they began walking toward the copse of trees. Voices caught his attention and he glanced back to see Locke and Portia, kneeling beside him.

"I shall miss our son and Portia. And the grandchildren."

"We'll check in on them from time to time. They're going to have wonderful lives."

He gazed down on her serene face. "How do you know? Another premonition?"

She smiled. "No, but you ensured they have a good foundation. You helped Locke learn to love. The residence is filled with warmth and joy again."

"And ticking clocks. That will no doubt drive Locke mad."

"At first perhaps, but he'll grow accustomed to it."

She was probably right. She tended to be right about everything. He didn't want to watch his children grieving—especially as there was no reason for sadness. At long last, he was with the woman he loved.

"What awaits us now?" he asked.

"I don't know, my love. I've been waiting for you before moving on. Shall we go exploring?"

Slipping his arm around her waist, he turned and began escorting her toward the trees, toward eternity. Never again would they be apart.

"I love you, Linnie," he whispered.

"As well you should, m'lord."

Laughing, he gathered her up in his arms, anxious to share with her the adventures that awaited them.

Havisham Hall

Killian St. John, the seventh Marquess of Marsden, claimed not to believe in ghosts, spirits, or hauntings. So it was an odd thing indeed for a man such as he to arrange for an orchestra to play in the balcony of the empty ballroom through the night in near darkness every Christmas Eve. No matter how chilly the weather, the doors to the ballroom were left open.

It was rumored, that on occasion, if one looked very closely with an open heart, one would see the faint silhouette of a couple waltzing in the moonlight that poured in through the windows and if one listened very carefully one would hear the tinkling of laughter followed by whispered words of love.

Keep reading for an exclusive excerpt to
New York Times bestselling author
Lorraine Heath's

AN AFFAIR WITH A
NOTORIOUS HEIRESS

The Marquess of Marsden always follows the rules. Expected from birth to adhere to decades of tradition, he plans to marry a proper young woman from a good family. But when a beautiful, and completely unsuitable, woman snags his heart, he begins to realize that to get what you want, sometimes you have to break the rules.

Linnie Connor dreams of the independence of running her very own bakery. And while she may be allowed to be a marquess' childhood companion, the baker's daughter never ends up with the handsome nobleman. Determined to achieve at least one of her dreams, Linnie makes plans to leave her sleepy village for London, intent on purging him from her heart. And yet, when an invitation to the Marsden annual ball arrives, she can't refuse her one chance to waltz in his arms.

It will be a night that stirs the flames of forbidden desires and changes their lives forever.

Available May 2017!

CHAPTER 1

London
1882

"Allow me the honor of introducing Lady Margaret Sherman..."

"Allow me to introduce Lady Charlotte..."

"...Lady Edith..."

"...Miss..."

"...Lady..."

The introductions of a new crop of debutantes became a blur of bright eyes, hopeful smiles, dangling dance cards, fluttering eyelashes, and waving fans. Yet Alistair Mabry, Marquess of Rexton, future Duke of Greystone, suffered through it all with gentlemanly aplomb, wishing to be anywhere other than where he was: his sister's infernal ball. Considering the mad crush of people who attended any affair hosted by the Duke and Duchess of Lovingdon, he was rather certain he wouldn't be missed—except by the mamas who considered him—at the age of nine and twenty—prime marriage material for one of their daughters, rather convinced he was in want of a wife despite the fact he had, on numerous occasions, indicated quite forcefully the opposite. His father was in good health. His mother had provided a spare, so Rexton was truly in no rush to become shackled.

He carried on polite conversations because Grace had asked him not to immediately disappear into the male-only domain of the card room. Once it became obvious senseless banter was all he was willing to grant, the ladies slowly drifted away like so many delicate petals on a summer breeze, dance cards minus his signature dangling from their limp wrists. Because he'd promised Grace an hour of his presence in the grand parlor and a mere forty minutes had passed, in order to stay true to his word, he wandered to a far corner populated with only ferns.

Watching the proceedings carried out before him, he couldn't deny that as much as he detested grand affairs, he was intrigued by the secretive games played, and it was to his benefit to remain in the good graces of the aristocracy because at some point, he would indeed be searching for a wife, one with an impeccable reputation, good breeding, and a penchant for staying out of the gossip sheets. While his own family had withstood numerous scandals, the process of deflecting censure was wearisome and he had no desire whatsoever to spend the remainder of his life serving as titillating fodder for the gossips. He'd made it a habit to be above reproach, which made him one of the more boring members among his family and friends, but it was advantageous to be

considered dull. He wasn't scrutinized very closely which meant he was free to do as he pleased within the shadows. And within the shadows, life was never dull.

"Lord Rexton."

He turned slightly, having no wish to offend the older man. Garrett Hammersley, an American by birth, had embraced England as his own when he moved to London in order to oversee his family's firearms operations. Opening a factory in England had allowed them to claim the business as an international venture, which had added significantly to their stock value. Their subsequent wealth had given him entry into the more elite circles. Their paths crossed from time to time, mostly at the horse races. He was in possession of something Rexton coveted, and his recent attempts to convince the man to part with it had disappointingly failed. "Hammersley."

"Say, old chap, I was wondering if I might bother you fo a tiny favor."

Rexton smiled inwardly. Favors usually came with a p The question was: Would Hammersley pay his? "Wha you have in mind?"

"My young niece, my dear departed brother's da has just had her coming out. Unfortunately, I need to help wash off the blemish of her scandalous old was hoping you'd be willing to step up to the task

Rexton knew the older sister only by reputat quite the splash when she arrived in London a f lier, she'd caught the eye of the Earl of Landsd fairy-tale courtship had captured the attention

ain. A few years after they wed, she had engaged in a notorious public affair that had left Landsdowne with no choice
except to divorce her, which had resulted in further scandal
because those in the aristocracy worth their salt simply did
not divorce under any circumstances. Knowing what it was to
be touched by scandal, he had empathy for the younger sister,
but he rather suspected teaching her to box wasn't going to
help her situation. "I don't really see how I can be of service."

Hammersley brushed his fingers over his thick sprinkled-
with-gray mustache, twice one way, twice the other. "You are
the most sought after bachelor in London, and have the respect of your peers. You're also known to have excellent taste
in women and horses. If you were to show some interest in
the girl—"

"I'm not looking to marry just yet." His compassion went
only so far.

"No, no, of course not. I don't expect you to lead her to
the altar. But if you were to dance with her, perhaps take her
on an outing to Hyde Park, be seen with her as it were, it
might serve to pique the other gents' curiosity. I'm certain
once they take an interest in her, they will be charmed as she
is a most charming girl. She has none of her sister's . . . flaws,
shall we say?"

Flaws? The inability to remain faithful? To publicly
cuckold her husband? To divorce a man whose lineage
could be traced back to William the Conqueror? Americans
certainly had a way of understating the faults of a calami-
tous woman. "I'm afraid you'll need to turn elsewhere for
assistance on this matter; ask another gent."

"Damn it, man, no one else has your influence. The younger swells work to emulate you. They'll follow your lead. Take some pity on the poor girl. I promised my brother on his deathbed I would see her well situated, and she's enamored of the nobility."

"So was her sister from what I understand."

"In temperament they are nothing alike. Mathilda was always too strong-willed to be ruled. But Gina, bless her heart, is a shy wallflower for whom hope springs eternal. I have to do something to spark awareness of her. And I've deduced you're the ticket."

Tickets came at a cost. "A dance, you say, and an afternoon at the park?"

"Not much more than that, I should think. Truly, she's a remarkable girl."

But not one who stood out if Hammersley had to approach Rexton regarding generating interest in her. He wasn't quite comfortable with the notion of giving the girl false hope regarding his intentions, but if he kept his interest casual perhaps no harm would be done. "Once I dance with her, mamas are going to think I've announced my stepping into the marriage market. It's going to create some inconvenience as I'll be fending off ladies for the remainder of the Season, which has only recently begun."

"I'll make it worth your while."

But was it fair to the girl? He'd do all in his power to bring a quick end to the farce and find a proper gent for her. "Oh? How might you go about that?"

"Black Diamond. You can take him to stud."

"Thrice."

"Damn it, man, do you know how valuable that stallion is?"

"I do indeed." Since the Arabian had soundly beaten Rexton's best stallion in several races. "I want at least three progeny off him."

"Two."

Which had been Rexton's price all along. "Two it is."

"But not until my niece has a viable suitor. You have to play at courting her until someone makes it a point to beat you."

That would be a further inconvenience, as he doubted many gents would even consider that they could beat him. His was one of the most powerful families in Great Britain. But to have Black Diamond breed with his Fair Vixen would be worth it. He had little doubt the mingling of those blood-lines would produce a champion. "Consider it done."

"Excellent. However, our agreement must remain be-tween us gentlemen. I don't want her hurt, so if it becomes known to her, our bargain becomes null and void."

He was well aware ladies had tender feelings. "I would expect no less."

"Come along then, let me introduce you to Gina. Who knows? You might just decide she's the one for you."

He seriously doubted that, but he was a man, after all, and ladies did interest him. "Should that happen, it won't nullify our agreement."

"Absolutely not. It will simply make our arrangement all the tidier."

A Letter from the Editor

Dear Reader,

I hope you liked the latest romance from Avon Impulse! If you're looking for another steamy, fun, emotional read, be sure to check out some of our recent and upcoming titles.

For fans of historical romance, we have a fabulous new male/male novel from Cat Sebastian! The Lawrence Browne Affair is a beautiful love story about an earl hiding from his future and a swindler haunted by his past. New York Times bestselling author Tessa Dare claims, "Cat Sebastian has a place on my keeper shelf!" . . . will she have a place on yours?

If you like rock stars, look no further than Havoc by Jamie Shaw! This novel is "romantic perfection" (New York Times bestselling author Rachel Harris) and features a sexy drummer who just wants to find The One. I dare you not to fall in love with Mike Madden and Jamie's amazing cast of characters in his band, The Last Ones to Know.

And last but not least, mark your calendar for the release of Christy Carlyle's next Victorian historical romance! *A Study in Scoundrels is the enchanting story of a proper English woman who moonlights as the mysterious author of popular detective novels . . . and her delicious romance with a scandalous actor! Christy's writing is witty, sexy, and wildly entertaining! Preorder it now and tell us what you think when it comes out next month.*

You can purchase any of these titles by clicking the links above or by visiting our website, www.AvonRomance.com. Thank you for loving romance as much as we do. Enjoy!

Sincerely,

Nicole

Editorial Director

Avon Impulse

LORRAINE HEATH always dreamed of being a writer. After graduating from the University of Texas, she wrote training manuals, press releases, articles, and computer code, but something was always missing. When she read a romance novel, she not only became hooked on the genre, but quickly realized what her writing lacked: rebels, scoundrels, and rogues. She's been writing about them ever since. Her work has been recognized with numerous industry awards, including RWA's prestigious RITA®. Her novels have appeared on the *USA TODAY* and *New York Times* bestseller lists.